D0669153

Publish and be damned
www.pabd.com

100 PERCENT EROTICA

by
Suzie van Aartman

Publish and be damned
www.pabd.com

First published in Canada 2006 by Suzie van Aartman.
The moral right of Suzie van Aartman to be identified as the author of this work has been asserted.

Designed in Toronto, Canada by Adlibbed ltd.
Printed and bound by Lightningsource in the US or the UK.

ISBN: 1-897312-30-X

Publish and be Damned helps writers publish their books. Our service uses a series of automated tools to design and print your book on-demand, eliminating the need for large print runs and inventory costs. Now, there's nothing stopping you getting your book into print quickly and easily.

For more information or to visit our book store please visit us at www.pabd.com

With thanks to Sue for reading the manuscript and for her constructive comments.

Also thanks to John for his advice and support.

CONTENTS

EARLY START

It was six o'clock on a wet, cold Saturday morning in November and I was pulling onto the works car park. I had left Rich snoring in bed and at this moment in time I wish I was still there with him. We had a rush job on at work and there was still a lot of packing to do so it could be ready for despatch first thing Monday. I didn't usually do Saturdays, but it was extra money and Christmas was just around the corner and Bill the foreman was very persuasive. A nice bloke of forty and divorced, but a bit shy and he let the management take advantage of him as did Pam and Chrissie whose dubious company I also had to endure this morning. They were both in their early twenties and thought they were God's gift to men and the only women in the world who could give good sex, or at least that's the impression they liked to convey. I was fifty five and they were always at pains to let me know that sex after fifty was disgusting and should be banned by law. Whether they intended to have their pussies sewn up for their fiftieth birthday remained to be seen. As for me I didn't broadcast my sexual desires from the rooftop but I was far from celibate and intended to be fucked for as long as the desire was with me.

I locked the car and shivered across the car park avoiding the puddles. The factory lights were on and reflected on the wet tarmac. Bill must have just arrived as I could hear the metallic ticking from his car engine as it was cooling down. No sign of Pam's car though. I entered and clocked on. Bill was wheeling a pallet of valves to the packing bench. That was today's labour.

'Morning Karen.'

'Morning Bill.'

'Pam has just phoned. They will be a bit late. She's had to knock Chrissie up.'

'Too many rum and blacks last night' I put in.

'Probably so.' Replied Bill lowering the pallet. 'Kettle's on.'

I went into the rest room and hung up my coat. Standing in front of the mirror I pulled my top straight. Not a bad figure for my age I thought as I ran my hands down my sides. Ample tits, even if they are sagging a bit

9

now. I leaned forward and inspected my cleavage which my top showed off very well, a cleavage I've noticed Bill ogling at, when I've been bending over a pallet. He always looks away quickly when I stand up, pretending he wasn't looking and not to embarrass him I pretend not to notice. His innocent admirations I find both flattering and exciting and many is the time I have been lying in the bath and fantasising about what might be. He always gave me a kiss on my birthday and at Christmas and the last one was bordering on passionate as I felt his tongue touch my lips in a very suggestive licking fashion. If only the boss had not been nearby; well who knows. Anyway still standing in front of the mirror I let my hands caress over my breasts and I could see my nipples becoming erect and showing through. I also noticed my straps needed adjusting as one breast was slightly higher than the other. I pushed my left breast up as I tried to pull the strap down the other side. As I did so Bill came in and his eyes immediately focused on my protruding nipples.

'Oh sorry Karen' He stammered, his cheeks taking on a light pinkness.

I found his innocence very refreshing compared to the coarseness of some of the others. In a situation like this Pam and Chrissie would have taken advantage and made him cringe with embarrassment.

'That's alright Bill, there's no need to apologise.'

I removed my hand from my breast and stroked his cheek. 'You're very sweet Bill.'

I found emotions stirring within me. Emotions which I knew should be suppressed but at the same time I found very exciting. I felt Bill's strong hand on mine and he kissed the palm of my hand gently. He had that look in his eye as we stood face to face. That look of power. He slid his arm around me and pulled me to him. His lips met mine. We looked into each others eyes and we knew. Gently taking my chin between his thumb and forefinger he opened my mouth and kissed me again. This time with a great desire, a desire that filled me with excitement, my fantasy was about to be fulfilled.

He clutched me with such emotion; I could feel the electric passion that was within his body. Passion that was unrestrained. His eager hands ran up and down my back, and then his hands clutched my buttocks pulling them wide apart and pulling me to his manhood. He was almost lifting me off the floor and I could feel his erection rubbing against my belly. I wanted him; I wanted him to take me here and now. His kissing was relentless and was taking on an increased urgency. His eager hand was now travelling slowly with restrained desperation up my side. I knew where it was going and I willed him on faster, but he was playing me like an angler plays a fish and was making me suffer so exquisitely. Take my tit you bastard, I thought to myself. Eventually after what seemed an eternity his hand arrived at its destination and I let out a loud sigh of ecstasy.

'Oh Bill, take me.' I murmured.

His hands slid up my back, under my top and with great expertise he unclipped my bra. I felt my tits swing free as with one easy movement my top and my bra were lifted over my head and flew somewhere across the room. Bill fell to his knees and began to worship my breasts, taking one in each hand and fondling them with great vigour. Then alternatively he took them in his mouth sucking my nipples so hard it almost hurt.

'They're beautiful.' he gasped, 'absolutely beautiful.'

I looked in the mirror, this mirror that started off this mornings events, and I watched Bill as he tried to devour my tits. As he continued to suck me his hands reached down to the clip of my slacks. He unfastened them and slowly unzipped them. And still sucking my breasts he reached round to my bottom and gripped my slacks and pants and slowly pulled them down over my buttocks. They fell to my ankles and I stepped out of them, kicking off my shoes at the same time. I stood naked before this kneeling, worshiping figure. It felt good, it was exciting, it was freedom and I felt powerful. Again I looked at the image in the mirror. This too was exciting, voyeuristic and exciting. Bill took my hips in his strong hands and kissed lower and lower until he reached my pubic mound.

I held out my hands to him and I urged him to stand. I unbuttoned his shirt and let it fall to the floor. He had a good physique, not perfect but respectable. He pulled me to him, my breasts pressing against his manly chest and he kissed me passionately again. I wanted more and I let my hands slide down until it found his manhood. His erection felt hard and wonderful within his trousers. I would give it its freedom. Undoing his garments as he had done for me I now kneeled before him and let them

11

slip to the floor. He slipped off his shoes and socks and he stood naked before my kneeling homage. I was in wonderment of his manhood. It was stiff as a ramrod and throbbing for attention. Probably all of eight inches long, thick shaft and a huge bulbous glans. I took it in my hand and I couldn't close my fist around it. I gently let my hand slide up and down its length. Bill moaned with pleasure. I had him at my mercy. I kissed the end of his cock which was now beginning to seep with his semen. I licked it off with a gentle lap of my tongue and holding it firmly I let him enter my mouth. Bill moaned with pleasure. Looking sideways into the mirror my mouth was fully open and I could only just take the end of his huge cock. But the image in the mirror was so incredibly stimulating, a huge cock being forced into my little mouth. I continued to suck him until I realised he was getting close to the point of coming and he took my shoulders and lifted me to my feet, his cock almost popping as it came out of my mouth.

'Your turn now.' He growled.

He sat me on the edge of the table and gently pushed me back. Kneeling down he lifted my legs and put them over his shoulders. He stared with mad lust in his eyes at my pussy making a low passionate moan. I was so excited I was willing my lips to open for him and take him inside. He kissed my knee and slowly kissed all along my inner thigh. I could feel my love juice pouring out of me as I willed him on faster but he knew how to tease. My pussy was quivering, almost aching for attention as his tongue got ever closer. He was nearly there and I slid my fingers down and pulled my lips open to receive his eager tongue. With a scream of relief he made contact with my clitoris. It was wonderful and he slowly and rhythmically licked me. His tongue moved down between my lips to my box and I could feel him enter me, probing me with his tongue. Then back up between my lips to my clit again and there he worked on me. It was exquisite and I knew very soon I would come. This was beautiful but I wanted to come with his cock inside me, I wanted to feel his shaft deeply thrusting inside my tight little cunt.

'Fuck me Bill, please fuck me.' I pleaded.

He didn't need asking twice. He got to his feet and lifted my legs high and wide. I felt his cock touching my lips and I reached down to guide it to its target. Bill knew he was in position and I could feel his huge cock sliding in. Again the mirror came to good use, as the image of yourself being fucked is unbelievably erotic. Bill's cock, inch by erotic inch slid inside me. It felt a very tight fit and I could see my lips stretching around his shaft. I felt it slide under my cervix and eventually reach the end of its journey. As he pulled back it glistened with my love juice as my lips seemed to suck it. Seven of his eight inches emerged and he started to travel inside me again. The rhythm picked up and his cock slid inside me faster and faster banging hard inside my cunt. It hurt a little but it was a nice hurt. Inevitably I could feel the climax coming and I could tell by the pain of ecstasy on Bill's face that he was ready too.

'Oh Bill, I'm coming.' I cried.

'So am I,' he said through gritted teeth.

We both exploded and screamed out in rapture simultaneously. I could feel his cock rippling inside me as simultaneously my cunt gripped him and sucked him further inside me. His hot cream shot inside my eager cunt and squelched out of me with his thrusting until I could feel it trickling over my bottom.

I lay there panting as Bill still held my legs and his shaft still inside me. I can honestly say that that was the best fuck of my whole life. I also noticed that there were two faces at the window. It was Pam and Chrissie with mouths wide open. They had watched this old lady of fifty five being fucked almost unconscious and that thought was almost as exciting as being fucked itself.

I did not tell Bill they were there and I heard them going into the ladies. So we got dressed and he was none the wiser. We later got on with the job and for once I have never known the two of them so quiet. They certainly didn't mention what they saw and they certainly didn't talk about their sexual forays. Perhaps that's all they could do, just talk.

A good day I think, and at time and a half as well.

THREE PLUS ONE

We were having one of those giggly girly evenings that you need every now and then, to let off steam and put the world to rights over a few bottles of wine. There was Claire, who was about thirty and a hairdresser. Lovely bubbly girl Claire, always laughing and messing about. She had shoulder length fair hair with a fringe, and a pretty face. Claire was a little bit plump but not excessively so, and she had two points about her that made her stand out from the crowd, because she was the proud owner of an enormous bosom. It was something that she was obviously very self conscious about and usually wore a jacket and walked with a stoop so not to draw attention to them. But their size was such that you could not help but notice them. Anyway this evening her inhibitions were somewhat subdued by half a bottle of white wine and she sat relaxing at the table with the two of us. Not consciously realising of course that the table was at such a height, she was able to rest her huge tits on it, which must have taken an incredible strain from her specially made reinforced bra.

The other member of the group was Linda a tall elegant lady with long black hair who was about forty but she still looked very attractive. Her husband Reg was something to do with finance and banking and they were very well off and she looked it.

And there was me, Yvonne who was ordinary in every way and supplied the wine and nibbles. As the wine took effect barriers of social grace became more relaxed and conversation ranged to a number of subjects but inevitably came to sex. I thought it a brilliant idea if the three of us could have a group session together. I knew that Linda had had a fling with another woman when Reg was away, and I had a curiosity about it myself. And Claire I knew had lots of boyfriends but she confided in me that they were only interested in her tits and after they had had their cocks between them they were off.

I needed something to get them in the mood before I broached the subject, so I got out the porno magazines that John had bought back from

14

Germany along with a selection of vibrators that have been accumulated over the years, as you do. I just dropped this lot on the table in front of them and waited for their reaction, which was immediate. Claire with a glazed expression on her face picked up my biggest vibrator which was about twelve inches long and ran her hand slowly up and down its knobbly length.

'Wow,' she gasped 'can you get all this inside you?'

'Not quite, but its great fun trying.' I said blushing slightly at the happy memories I had from it.

Claire continued stroking the huge shaft and was obviously captivated by it. You could tell by her manner that she was mentally fucking herself with it. We are going to have fun later with that I thought to myself.

Meanwhile Linda was pouring over the pictures in the magazines.

'Look at that.' She said 'Talk about mutual masturbation.'

It was a picture of one woman lying on a bed with her legs open and knees bent. A second woman was kneeling either side of her head leaning forward with her face between her legs licking her clitoris. She in turn was being licked by the woman below, who judging by how she was gripping the top woman's buttocks was on the verge of coming. You could not really see any intimate details being photographed from side on, but the image it conveyed to Linda seemed to be electric. Her nipples were standing proud from her sweater so she was obviously excited, which also excited me.

We all moved through to the lounge taking all the goodies with us and sat on the settee. Claire in the middle and Linda and me either side of her. She still hadn't let go of the vibrator and was clutching it like a child with a favourite doll. Linda on the other side seemed more interested in the pictures and when she saw one that especially titillated her she would whoop and show us. One she found was of particular cause for comment. It was of a woman about to take a cock into her mouth. The cock was huge and must have been at least as big as Claire's vibrator, or even bigger. She had only got his bell end in her mouth and that was a very tight fit. In the next picture she had taken the whole length. Now it was either a trick photo, or she had his cock going down her throat or as

Linda suggested 'she must have a hole at the back of her head.'

Either way it was an incredible sight. On the next page he had come and his come was all over her face and dripping from his cock. There was a huge amount of it and I had never known any man produce that much come in one go.

Claire was also excited by the pictures and she seemed to be unconsciously working the vibrator up and down with her hand. I caught Linda's eye and as if our eyes spoke for us we both leaned forward in front of Claire and kissed each other longingly and meaningfully.

'What about me?' Said Claire.

With that I kissed Claire pushing my tongue into her mouth. She moaned with pleasure. At the same time Linda stood up and took all her clothes off standing naked watching us. I paused and without opening her eyes Claire lay back and sighed. I stood with the naked Linda and we kissed. I felt her hand creeping up my side and squeezed my tit. I had no bra on and I could feel her playing with my nipple. She didn't waste any time and put both her hands inside my shirt and ripped it open sending buttons showering everywhere. My tits were naked and free. I unzipped my jeans, kicked them away and flung off my knickers. It felt strangely liberating to be standing naked with another woman. We hugged and kissed and I took her tits in my mouth and sucked and sucked.

On the settee Claire gave a moan of pleasure as she watched us fondling and kissing each other. She was obviously turned on as she had her hand up her skirt and in her knickers and she was fingering herself. We pulled her to her feet and started to undress her. Linda slipped her jumper over her head and I took her skirt off. As she stood in her underwear you had to admire her figure. She had nice wide hips and her legs where a good shape, but her crowning glory were those huge tits straining to get out of that bra. Linda went behind her and unclipped it, then gently eased the straps from her shoulder pulling down gently letting her bra fall to the floor. They were a magnificent sight and far from sagging to her waist as you might expect they stuck out very firmly, and they must have stuck out at least twelve inches. I stood breathless staring at them. Linda reached round from behind and took them in her hands and you could tell by how she handled them that they were very firm. Each nipple was at least an inch across and the disc around them was dark and measured about six inches. I kneeled before her to worship her tits sucking those purple nipples and burying my face in her tit flesh.

The door bell rang. Linda looked through the window to see who it was.

'There's a gorgeous bloke at the door' she said. 'Let's have him in and have some fun with him.'

I reluctantly removed my face from Claire's tits and looked out. It was Dave from next door. He was indeed gorgeous and recently separated. I thought what the hell, he might like some fun and I bet he never found himself in a situation like this. I put on my buttonless shirt and went to the door.

I led him into the living room and when he saw Linda his jaw dropped. When he saw Claire's huge tits I thought his eyes were going to drop out. Dave has a headache I told them and has come round for a couple of aspirins. He stood transfixed as I got the tablets and a glass of wine to wash them down.

'Take two of these.' I told him. And he obeyed. I massaged his shoulders as he sipped the wine. 'You are all tense Dave. That's what has caused your headache. You need relief.'

'Well those aspirins will do the trick.' He said nervously, not quite being able to believe the situation he was in.

'They weren't aspirin Dave.' I said teasingly.

'What were they?'

'Viagra.' And the girls giggled.

'Viagra.' He said startled. 'You are only supposed to take one aren't you?'

'Yes, but you've got a heavy session ahead of you Dave.' Added Linda.

'I think his head ache has gone anyway.' Piped up Claire, caressing her breasts and pointing them towards Dave.

I let my hands slide from his shoulders, down his back and clutched his tight buttocks.

'Nice arse Dave.'

'Thanks.' He said nervously.

I reached around the front and I could feel he had a hard on.

'My word that Viagra works fast.' I said.

'Well let's not waste it then.' Said Claire unfastening his jeans and removing them and his shorts and trainers, simultaneously and with great skill.

Linda whipped off his T shirt and apart from his white socks he was as naked as the rest of us.

I pushed the pouf in front of the armchair, Linda sat him on it and I pushed him back to lie on the seat of the armchair. His giant cock stood up like a pulsating periscope and Claire, who for the first time this evening had put down the vibrator said in a girlish voice 'Me first.'

With that she straddled him, took the giant cock and guided it into her eager little cunt as she lowered herself on him. She moaned with pleasure as it entered her right up to the hilt. She rode him like a stallion; she had her feet on the ground and her hands on the arms of the chair and she was in complete control. Moving her hips back and forth she made his cock work the inside of her cunt while her clitoris rubbed against his pubic bone. It was a remarkable sight and I reached for the video camera, this has got to be recorded for posterity and a good giggle later. Claire continued to fuck him like a trooper her huge tits were bouncing up and down like giant melons. As for Dave, well the Viagra was certainly working.

The chair they were using was adjustable, so I let the backrest down so it was flat. This bought an eager Linda into play and she was able to kneel either side of Dave's head and lower her eager clitoris over his mouth which he licked eagerly sending Linda into little screams of ecstasy. I eagerly carried on filming this orgy from various angles. I took a close up from behind Claire creating a beautiful image of her cunt lips sucking Dave's huge cock. And from behind Linda a close up of Dave's tongue licking her lips and teasing her clitoris. Linda also supported herself with the help of Claire's enormous tits. Not only support but pleasure as well for all three of us.

Eventually the two girls had their fill and both screamed out in orgasm almost simultaneously. They both got off exhausted. Dave's cock was glistening with Claire's love juice but was still hard and stiff. His face was flushed and his cheeks were wet with Linda's succulence. It was now my turn and I gave Linda the camera. I looked at that glistening cock and knelt down beside it taking it in my mouth. I could taste Claire and that gave me an extra thrill. I worked his cock up and down in my mouth and I could feel him responding, I could feel his cock tightening. As I knelt there I felt a buzz in my cunt. It was Claire she had turned the vibrator on and was about to shove it in me. I felt my lips part and the huge vibrator sinking deeply into my cunt. She handled it expertly as she pushed it in and out, slowly at first then gradually faster. Only a woman truly knows what a woman wants, and Claire knew what I wanted. On and on she went getting faster and faster the vibrations making my cunt cry out for more. I could feel myself coming and started to breathe heavily. Claire sensed me coming as did Dave. My cunt gripped the vibrator and Claire sensed this. At the same time Dave's cock pulsated like the vibrator in my cunt and his come shot into my mouth like a pulsating hosepipe. It was hot and creamy and oozed out like a volcano erupting. At the same time my cunt erupted and I screamed out 'I'm coming' as Dave's cream oozed from my mouth.

What a session that was, and what a film it was. I got it on the computer later and made a copy for each of us. Dave was in awe of the effects of the Viagra. I hadn't the heart to tell him it was just aspirin and that his great performance was due simply to the power of suggestion. Which just goes to demonstrate the power of the mind. If you believe strongly enough, you can do almost anything, within reason of course.

A QUIET NIGHT IN

It was Friday at last, it had been a long long week and I was glad it was over. It was nearly eight o'clock when I got home and I was going to have a shower and maybe open a bottle of wine and microwave a ready meal. John was still away on business and I missed him greatly. The evenings were always the time of day that I felt his absence most. Not only was it his company I missed but also his body. Sex with him was always interesting and exciting, we had been together for over five years and there were no signs of the lustre losing its shine.

I walked through the living room, kicking off my shoes, dropped my jacket on the settee, my handbag on the armchair and on through to the kitchen. Picking a wine glass from the shelf, corkscrew from the drawer and bottle of chardonnay from the fridge. With a reassuring pop the wine was open and glugged into my glass. The first mouthful is always the best. I thought for a moment about those wine tasting experts and how they deciphered between each sort of wine, and even the year they were made. To my mind wine was wine and if it tasted OK and didn't cost an arm and a leg it was good enough for me. In fact that's probably the case with most people and a lot of these so called pretentious wine prats that you hear rabbiting on about wine at parties and such like are just that, pretentious prats.

The warm water from the shower felt very invigorating, it was one of those power showers and it made the whole body tingle. Looking at myself in the mirror I could see the setting sun was catching the spray making it look like an orange aura surrounding my body. I could also see that I was developing a bit of a paunch and that a few vigorous sessions at the gym were called for. But on the whole I wasn't in too bad a shape. My tits were in good condition, and I always heeded my mother's advice and wore a good supporting bra.
'Too many of these women's liberators have ended up with their bosoms around there knees by the time they are forty because of not wearing bras' she used to preach.
I was glad of that advice because I was only five foot one and had a

20

very full forty two inch bust. So with the passage of time, the effects of gravity, my tits would have probably been around my knees as well. Anyway I was thirty with no kids and a good bra so my tits or melons as John called them looked pretty good, in fact looking in the mirror as the water cascaded over them they looked very good. And as I massaged the shower gel over them they glistened and shone as the setting sun highlighted them. They were indeed a pair to be proud of, and they certainly caught the eyes of that randy lot in the office.

The massaging of my tits was quite erotic and with that and the stimulation from the water, it was making my nipples very erect. In fact I could almost hang the plastic hook of the shower gel bottle from them. I didn't though as that would be somewhat disrespectful of such 'icons of eroticism,' John's words not mine. I looked at myself in the mirror. I held my stomach in and pushed my chest out.

Yes not bad at all, I thought. Placing my hands on my chest I let them follow the contours of my body. My tits were indeed very large and quite firm and I let my hands caress their contours. Pushing them up and letting them go they fell back into place after a brief tantalising wobble. John liked to see me doing this sort of thing; his favourite was watching me rubbing talc into them. I did it in front of the mirror on the landing and from the bed I could see him watching me. So I used to massage them to greater effect, making them shake as much as I could. It always turned him on and we had great sex afterwards. The water cascaded over my tits and dripped from my nipples. They too were pretty large and even with a good bra and a thick sweater they would show through if I got excited. And the areola discs, surrounding the nipples were tantalisingly dark and nearly four inches across.

The top half done I turned my attention to my lower half. I ran my soapy hands around my crutch and bum. My thoughts again turning to John and the many happy evenings we had. I let my fingers run between my lips and gently stroke my clitoris it was very exciting and I felt in need of some sexual relief. Not here I thought, so I quickly dried myself and made for the bedroom, closed the curtains and turned on the light. I sat naked on the bed and reached into my top drawer where I kept my girly things. I found the love letters that John had sent me over the years, they were always good to read again when I was alone and feeling a bit low. Not only were they romantic they were also very erotic, some bordering on the pornographic in fact. And also our album of naughty pictures. Oh the joy of digital photography and delayed action cameras. There were some very good shots. In one of them I am lying on my side and John is behind me holding my leg up high and with his cock stuck right up inside me, and at the same time I am fingering my clitoris. That was a brilliant picture, and a brilliant fuck too, because when the camera went off I was climaxing and it shows by the expression on my face. In another shot I am lying on the bed and John is in a kneeling position holding my ankles at his shoulder level with my legs wide open, in fact I am almost doing the splits and John's shaft is inside me as far as it will go. These images were really getting me going and my pussy was soaked in love juice. I needed satisfying. I rummaged deeper in my girly drawer and found my vibrator. Twelve inches of ecstasy. I guided it into my eager slit with it on full blast and pushed it up until it almost hurt. I was leaning against the headboard of the bed holding these two pictures in front of me fantasising about being fucked by John. As I shoved my plastic vibrating dick in and out and as far up as I could get it I thought about John's warm stiff cock inside me. After a few minutes eager thrusting I pulled it out and started to suck it. It was still vibrating and it made a tickling sensation in my mouth. As I sucked back and forth on it I could taste my juice and it made me feel like it was John's cock as one of the things he liked was to fuck me for a few minutes and then for me to suck him till he came. This is what I visualised, John's throbbing cock in my mouth. I felt it tighten and heard him moan. Then he let out a cry and I felt the pulsating of his knob as his hot come filled my eager mouth and I swallowed the lot. It was almost as though I could feel his come going down my throat. In reality John would have rolled over a spent force, but the plastic technology was still game for it and I shoved John's imaginary cock deep into my cunt again, thrusting once more with eagerness. Still looking at the pictures of John and me I could feel his mighty cock fucking me for all he was worth.

Holding the image in my mind I put the pictures down and with my free hand I fingered my clit. I was thrusting the vibrator in and out with one hand and fingering my clitoris with the other. It was wonderful and soon I exploded with a loud cry of 'I'm coming.'

It seemed to go on forever and I could feel John coming again shooting his hot come inside me and filling my cunt like he filled my mouth. It was beautiful the best fuck I have ever had. Maybe when John gets back we could film it.

ROUTINE IS A FUNNY THING

Routine is a funny thing. I had been working for J.J Warrender & Sons for seventeen years, in fact ever since Bob passed away. I remember Jane telling me after his funeral that 'I must look at this as a turning point in life, not the end of life itself.' I never really understood what she meant by that statement but I get the impression that I shouldn't mope about past life but start afresh. 'Get out and meet people, get a job.' I was thirty five then and still young and desirable they all told me. Seventeen years later and I'm still alone. Not so young and not so desirable and those statements of yesteryear sound very faint now on the winds of time. But now I'm nearly fifty three and much much older and my shape has also changed somewhat, as it invariably does. My bust is larger, in fact much much larger, but alas time and gravity have taken their toll. Still, looking in the bathroom mirror and holding my stomach in and the strategic placement of hands to help it stay in, I could look presentable, at least for as long as I could hold my breath.

As I say routine is a funny thing I was about to leave, as I did every day at four thirty for work. I arrive at five o'clock after all the production staff and most of the office staff had left. Harking back at Jane and friend's advice, this cleaning job wasn't really what I had envisaged. I didn't meet many people as most had left before I had arrived, and the remainder had the thought of leaving, uppermost in their minds. However it was a job and it filled the early part of my evenings. It was just routine, so I stuck with it. In my routine I was always sure to set up the video machine to record the Soaps and upon my return from work, that took care of the latter part of my evenings.

The job was invariably the same; I started by cleaning the factory toilets, then the tea rooms and the sinks full of mugs and plates etc.
'Good night Carol' called out Joe as he bustled past.
'Night Joe. Are you going to the ma....?' But too late he was gone.
At about six thirty the production area was usually completed and I started on the administration section, reception area first. Then the routine took me through to the offices.

Mr. Grocott the production manager was invariably still working. Planning tomorrows schedule or something of the like I imagine. He was always the last to leave as he was the key holder and it was his responsibility to lock up. He too, was a person of routine and all the years I have been there his routine never seemed to waver. A pleasant man, I guessed who was in his early sixties. Quite tall and slim with a good head of almost white air. He always wore a dark pin striped suit which gave him something of the air of a bank manager, and I'm ashamed to admit, not a bad looking bank manager at that.

I never knew what his personal circumstances were as he never encouraged personal conversation. Now don't get me wrong he was never strict or aloof, it's just I got the impression of rather a shy vulnerable man. Anyway as routine dictated I made him a cup of tea and took it in to him. His was rather a grand and spacious office as probably befits his station. His desk was on a slightly raised up area of the floor, almost like a nine inch stage. It was one of those things you always noticed in life but never really knew why and were always reluctant to ask, so I naturally thought it was to accommodate a stair well beneath or something of that nature.

I came in with his tea and approached his desk and stumbled slightly on the raised step of his desk area. Why I was so clumsy I do not know, after all I had been doing this for seventeen years. Quick as a flash Mr. Grocott was on his feet to steady me. There was no real need to, as I wasn't going to fall. But all the same he cupped my hands with his. Was it to save me or his tea I thought? Anyway for a moment our eyes met and I was drawn in.

'Are you alright?' He enquired in his deep but soft voice.

'Oh yes, I'm so sorry Mr. Grocott' I croaked half embarrassed and half excited.

He took his tea and sipped it still looking into my eyes.

'Mmm lovely as usual' he purred.

Then I did something really stupid. I stepped back and stumbled off the step and fell flat on my back. I was not hurt, just shaken and felt even more stupid about my clumsiness. What must this man think of me? It

25

shook me and it was a second or two before I composed myself. I must have looked a fool; I was on my back with my legs everywhere. I caught Mr. Grocott's expression. It was one of concern and wonderment, his jaw open. Then I realised. I was wearing self supporting stockings and French knickers. They were very comfortable to wear but in the position I was in, legs waving everywhere he must have had a real eye full of my pussy. He quickly but his cup down and came to my aid and pulled me to my feet and held me. I felt such a fool again and even more embarrassed knowing he had seen me so intimately. Then I thought what the hell I don't suppose it was the first pussy he had ever seen and what is more no one had seen it for seventeen years anyway. In those few seconds many thoughts ran through my mind. What did it matter what he saw. He was obviously a gentleman and would not bandy such gossip about the office. And in a strange sort of way I felt excited about it. For once I had done something that had interested a man, albeit accidentally, and that thought gave me a tingle. Not only a tingle in my heart but a tingle in my quim. I was aware of my lips becoming moist and at the same time I could feel my face becoming very red.

I was still in Mr. Grocott's arms.

'Are you alright Carol?' He uttered, genuinely concerned.

'Oh Mr. Grocott, I feel such a fool' I stammered, and assured him that I wasn't hurt.

'Phil.'

'Sorry?'

'My name is Phil. Only the bank manager calls me Mr. Grocott.'

After all these years I never knew his first name, I felt such a fool again.

'I see. Thank you Phil,' I said clumsily.

I found myself staring into his eyes and I was captivated. He was still holding me and I could feel his hand caressing my shoulder. Something was happening here and I was both excited and nervous at the same time. I felt also that I may be getting into deep water. I stammered out some stupid question about his wife's occupation and I felt like biting my tongue out after such an unimaginative conversation starter. However it transpired that he and she had divorced many years earlier. This was a different prospect and I felt myself feeling more relaxed.

There was a silence as he gazed into my eyes. I could feel a passion building but I also still felt a little uncertain.

'A pretty overall' he commented, looking down.

'It's nothing special' I replied also looking down at myself and seeing that my nipples were erect and sticking out very noticeably.

Phil held me closer. I thought, hang my inhibitions and let nature take its course and enjoy it. Our lips met and I felt myself dissolve into his arms. I could feel the electricity in his body and I knew he wanted me and I wanted him. He held me close and kissed so passionately that I felt like I was floating. His tongue gently eased its way into my mouth and he licked the tip of my tongue very erotically. I felt myself gently gripping his tongue and sucking it, moving my head gently backwards and forwards in a gentle thrusting motion. This seemed to excite him and I could feel him grip my body more firmly. I could not believe after all this time that a man was paying sexual attention to me, but what I did know was that I wanted what he was giving me.

His hands gradually slid down my back and in each hand he cupped my buttocks fondling and manipulating, then pulling them apart. I could feel the gusset of my knickers sliding between my now very wet lips. This man certainly knew what he was doing and he caressed between my buttocks with his finger and even fully clothed it felt very erotic. Again he began to fondle my buttocks pulling me closer to him and I could feel his erection pressing against my tummy as he rhythmically pulled me against his manhood.

Pausing for breath he undid my overall and let it fall to the floor.

There was a small settee in his office and with an indication with his hand he bade me to sit down and he sat down on my left. He continued with his passionate kissing, his arm around my waist. It was not long before his hand slowly travelled up my side. I knew where it was heading and I mentally yearned him to hurry up. Eventually his hand gently caressed my breast and with this, his kissing took on another level of passion, his tongue thrusting like a rampant penis. Harder and harder he fondled my breast and he kissed and licked my throat getting lower and lower, down my chest until he reached where his hand was. His mouth and tongue then took over sucking my breast and licking and gently nibbling my nipple. He then gave the same attention to my other breast and then very expertly undid my blouse with his left hand. He kissed my throat again and his hands gently slid my blouse from around my shoulders and tossed it into the room. In a smooth single movement he unclipped the back of my bra and sitting up straight he watched as he gently peeled it from me letting my breasts fall free. He gasped and just stared in wonderment.

'My God Carol they are wonderful' he said with his eyes like organ stops.

I gave a self conscious giggle. 'Sagging a bit now' I said.

He took one in each hand and gently caressed them. 'They are perfect. A good size and very firm.'

I felt very flattered by his comments and he continued his worship by thrusting his face between my tits kissing them and sucking my nipples with great vigour.

I pulled his head up and kissed him and he took me in his arms again. I felt his hand on the outside of my right thigh and it inevitably travelled up to where my stockings ended and flesh started. It then travelled down and across to my left knee. Its journey then was to be more passionate along the inside of my thigh.

'Oh Carol, open your legs for me' he pleaded.

I willingly obliged and it was not long before his hand reached their goal. I gasped with pleasure as his fingers caressed my pussy. I dearly wanted this man and all he had. His fingers easily slid under the gusset of my knickers and expertly his finger worked its way between my now very wet lips until it found my clitoris and he played it well. So well in fact I had to beg him to stop as it was too nice.

He stood up and he silently removed his clothes. His tie went somewhere to the left his shirt and socks somewhere to the right. His trousers dropped to the floor and were kicked away. I too stood up and unzipped my skirt and let it fall to the floor. He stood almost drooling at my naked breasts and my French knickers complete with self supporting stockings. I've never been able to fathom what it is about this combination that inflames men so much, I'm just glad it does. As I walked towards him I could feel my tits moving and felt his desire as he watched them. I could also see the bulge of his erection within his shorts. I stroked my breasts as I stepped towards him and pushing them into his chest. I then put my finger tips into his waist band and slipped down his pants which fell around his ankles. I took his shaft in my hands and rubbed it gently. It was warm, large and stiff. Still caressing him I kissed his chest. Then gradually kissed lower and kneeled before him. He stroked my hair and still holding his shaft I took it in my mouth. I gently sucked it in a rocking movement backwards and forwards taking it in as far as I could and then pulling back sucking all the way. I could tell from his moans that it was giving him great pleasure. So I continued by licking and kissing the end of his shaft then inserting his great length in and out.

He then stooped me before he got to the point of no return and took me by the arms and stood me up. With a wave of his arm he literally cleared his desk, leapt over to the settee removed their cushions plus one from a single chair and placed them on the desk. I went to remove my French knickers.

'No, don't take them off,' he commanded.

He came to me and put his right arm around my waist and his left behind my thighs and carried me to the desk and laid me gently on the cushions. My legs overhung the desk and he supported them until he moved to the end of the desk and kneeled with my legs resting on his shoulders. Slowly and methodically he kissed the inside of my thighs getting closer and closer. He gently kissed the gusset of my knickers and taking the initiative I simply pulled it to one side. At the same time I held my lips open so he could get inside me. He was so excited I thought he was going to eat me. He licked me with such vigour it was unbelievable. He ran his tongue between my lips down to my tunnel of love then inserted his tongue in an unbelievable distance. Then he licked my lips the other way until he reached my clitoris. Licking it up and down and round and round. The sensation was unbelievable. He kept on and on and on and I could feel the pleasure building. He then put his lips over

29

my clitoris and sucked and that was absolutely incredible. I felt myself coming like I've never felt before. It was like a volcano building up and he timed his sucking to perfection and I just couldn't hold it any longer and just screamed 'I'm coming' and then screamed some more. It was unbelievable. It seemed to go on for ever and Phil kept on sucking me.

He seemed to sense that he had given me his all and now it was his turn. He stood up still holding my legs and moved forward. I reached down and took his shaft and guided it into my quim. It didn't need much encouragement and he thrust it deep inside me. He lifted my legs high and wide and being in a standing position he had complete control and I could feel him going really deep inside me, even past my cervix. It was a wonderful sensation I was lying comfortably with a huge shaft inside me being fucked like I had never been fucked before. The fact I still had knickers on seemed to give Phil an extra turn on and as he fucked me I could feel him caressing the silky material of my knickers like a child getting comfort from a favourite silky blanket.

Harder and harder he thrust and faster and faster and I could tell from his heavy breathing he was close to coming.

'Oh God' he blurted as he gasped his pleasure.

I felt the unmistakable ripple of his shaft and the gush of his hot cream as I knew he had come inside me.

As he stood there panting I sat up and embraced him and we stood together arm in arm.

'Will you put those knickers on again for me next time?' He said.

'Certainly' I said. And the next time wasn't long coming. And there were many next times. And in six months time we were Mr. and Mrs. Grocott. And I can heartily recommend being fucked on a desk in French knickers and self support stockings. I would defy any man to resist.

A PLEASANT LIE IN

I awoke with that feeling you only get when you know that you haven't got to get up and go to work. It was made better knowing that it was Wednesday and everyone else was still hard at it. We had been busy lately with a big order that was now complete and out of the door and I wanted a day with Sue just to chill out.

It was a warm sunny morning in early summer, the sun was cascading through the open window and the gentle breeze was caressing my face. Lying there looking at the ceiling I thought how good life was and how lucky I was to have a wife like Sue. She gave a contented sigh as she began to wake up and quietly whispered 'I love you.' Our hands touched and I took hers in mine and gently squeezed it.

Being a warm night we only had a single cotton sheet on the bed and its sheerness outlined her gorgeous body to perfection. I could see clearly the contours of her firm young breasts with beautifully formed erect nipples that heaved slowly up and down as she breathed. I squeezed her hand again and she gently squeezed it back then pulled it onto her thigh. She then rubbed it gently inside her thigh going higher and higher. It seemed to take ages just to move just a few inches. It was her way of turning me on, knowing what I was going to get, but making me wait for it. The single cotton sheet was taking on another contour as my shaft was becoming rock hard and was standing up like a flagpole.

After what seemed an interminable time my hand finally reached its goal and we both let out a moan of pleasure as my fingers stroked her pussy. I let my fingers run between her lips down towards her tunnel of love and let my middle finger slide inside her. She was very wet and panting with excitement. I slide another finger inside her and waving them about made her even more eager. She pulled me over and pushed my head down to kiss her breasts. Although a having a very trim figure she had larger than average breasts which were very taught and firm and when she wore her tight T shirts with no bra she looked a treat. She pushed her breasts up and together and I submersed my face in them, if ever there was a good place to die this was it. As I sucked and nibbled her cherry like nipples I let my finger slide between her lips until I found her clitoris. She gasped as I gently stroked it and sucked her tits at the same time.

'Oh it's too nice' she moaned in ecstasy, and with that she pulled me on top of her and without any effort my shaft went in.

'Fuck me Steve. Fuck me slow and hard' she begged.

She not only looked beautiful she felt beautiful as well. Her cunt was a fantastic, indescribably pleasurable paradise that nothing in the world matched. It felt warm, moist and inviting and she had an incredible skill of making it contract so it felt tight and almost as if she was sucking me. It was so incredible it was almost impossible to keep fucking her for long without coming.

She reached down and grasped my buttocks and when I pushed my shaft into her tight little cunt she pulled me in further. It seemed to go in another two inches and I could feel my cock slide under her cervix. I could not go on for much longer and I knew that soon that feeling of orgasm would start.

'Oh Sue, it's too much' I begged.

'Lick me Steve, lick me.'

I withdrew and kneeled by her left side and leaned over her open legs. Her cunt was there inviting me back to give it more attention, the lips quivering and partly open. Glistening and soaked with love juice it wanted more attention. As I leaned forward to lick her clitoris, her hands slid down to pull open her lips which made her clitoris stand clear so I could easily get at it. She gasped as my tongue made contact. I let it slide down between her lips to her cunt then pushed my tongue inside. Then sliding back up I gave all my attention to her clitty. Backwards and forwards and round and round went my tongue and within a few minutes I could feel the signs that she was coming. Her hips gyrated and she held her breath. Then she let forward a moan that got louder and louder and turned into a scream. Her hands clutched my shoulder and her nails dug into my flesh. Her hips jerked up and down and I clutched her buttocks as I licked her harder, I wanted to keep her going as long as I could.

'Suck me, oh God suck me.' She ordered and I took her clitty in my lips and sucked. This seemed to make her come with renewed vigour and her hips continued to thrust. At the same time she reached through my legs with her left hand and grasped my cock and stated to jerk me off. She pulled at my thigh with her other hand.

'Get your leg over me quickly'

This I did, and kneeled either side of her head. Still rubbing my cock and pulling down at the same time I opened my legs wider to get lower and I could feel her guiding my cock into her mouth. I was sucking her and she was sucking me. As her orgasm died down I could feel mine begin to take hold and build and build until I could hold it no longer. I moaned with pleasure and I could feel my shaft tighten. She realised too and started jerking me harder and faster until I could feel my come shoot into her mouth. I heard her sigh and felt the movement of her cheeks as she sucked out the last remnants of come from my still throbbing cock and swallowed it.

I rolled over and turned to lie with her. I kissed her and stuck my tongue in her mouth and could taste myself. We fell asleep in each others arms. It definitely beats work.

ONE DAY

At last together are we.
Our clothes just dissolved away.
Arm in arm we stand naked and free.
Upon my knees I do descend
Your breasts to worship and adore
To kiss them and caress them
And to do much more
I sit you down upon the bed
And lay you back a passion to be fed
With pleasure and with sighs
Between your knees I kneel and kiss your thighs
Before me like two converging roads that lead to the centre of the
universe
Pure white flesh I kiss higher and higher
Until our lips meet, for that kiss so intimate
Oh ecstasy on fire, so it would
That sweet, intimate and erotic kiss
My tongue explores and tantalizes your womanhood
Up and down and round and round and on and on
To give you pleasure, with passion that is full on
A feeling building ever onwards until it reaches a volcanic climax
Slowly and with rhythm until your desire is satisfied
Your whole being consumed by that body gripping surge of pleasure
Not yet finished, like a spirit above you and upon you, I do descend
My Staff finds your Venus, that tunnel of love full of delights
And thrusts with energy
We are united as one; flesh enters flesh thrusting rhythmically until
the pleasure is too much to bear
Oh, dear lady you inflame me with such hot passion
Until at last we come together, consumed with ecstasy.
With love and sensuous tingles,
A final flood of pleasure, our love juice mingles
In the midst of the mist of love a cascade of erotic delight
Forbidden fruit tastes so sweet. Or so I'm told
We must try it for ourselves, before we get too old

TEAM PHYSIO

I stood on the balcony of the gymnasium watching the final moments of the match. The referee blows the whistle and it was all over, we had won. The club started at the bottom of the league and we finished at the top. Throughout the season they had performed well and not just on the pitch and I felt a tingle of pride knowing that my skills as a physio and mentor had gone a long way to securing victory. As I said I felt a tingle of pride but I also felt another tingle, a tingle of knowing that the ultimate sexual experience was soon to take place. I had promised the team that if they won the league every one of them could fuck me. As they triumphantly marched to the box to receive the cup some of them looked up and waved to me, blatantly clutching their man-sized manhood's and shouting 'We love you Liz.' Whatever the lady mayor thought I cannot imagine, no doubt it gave her a tingle in her pussy as well. Anyway they were mine this afternoon.

As they went through the necessary protocol and interviews I reflected back on the season and our dedicated work. We were only a provincial team of a provincial town, whose name I shan't disclose as most of the team were married and I'm sure the wives would not relish their extra sexual activities being made public. As a small club they could not afford a full time physiotherapist so as a lover of the game and men, it was a labour of love and I gave my services and extra services free.

I remember Garry coming to see me at the club, complaining of a stiffness from which he could get no relief. I had just got out of the shower and had a towel wrapped around me. He had emerged from the changing room and had only his football shorts on. It was not a regular training day but as he was not due at work until two o'clock he thought he would spend an hour in the gym. So there was just the two of us in the building.

'Just lie on the couch and I'll see what I can do.'

He lay there on his front, chin resting on his folded arms and I went to the cupboard for my rubbing oil. An aromatic preparation guaranteed to sooth aches and give sensual relief.

'How's you love life Garry?' I said just making conversation.

'Oh, err, fine thanks.' He said somewhat taken aback with the question.

'A fine fit specimen like you must give Donna a good time.'

'Well I've had no complaints.' He said obviously now a bit more relaxed.

I started to rub the oil into the back of his neck, upper back and shoulders. It was just as invigorating for me as for the patient. Those firm taut muscles and that manly aroma of fresh sweat. They were almost as effective as the massage.

'You're on the late shift this week then?'

'Yes.' He said almost as a sigh.

'It must be nice not having to get up at the crack of dawn.'

'Yes, not so nice when you're stuck at work till ten though.'

'Donna working today?'

'No, she's got the day off. In fact she is having one of her cleaning purges, that's why I've got out of her way.'

'Still lying in bed together must be nice.'

'Not when she is giving you the itinerary for the day.'

'You should have given her a good fucking. That would have shut her up.'

'What?' He said somewhat shocked at my forwardness.

'A good stiff cock thrust between her legs, that would have done the trick.'

He did not reply, just gave a nervous clearing of the throat.

I had worked my massage down across the middle of his back and was now concentrating on his lower back. Garry gave a moan.

'That's where it has been troubling me. My lower back.'

'You know what the trouble is don't you?'

'What?'

'Too much beer and not enough exercise. Your trouser belt has been digging in; I can see the marks.'

'Well what should I do about it?'

'Loosen your belt or even take it off.'

'But my trousers will slip down.'

'Better still. In fact take them of completely and give Donna a good seeing to as often as you can.'

I realised I needed some more oil so I went to the cupboard and reached up. As I did so I could feel my towel give way and it fell to the ground. 'Oops' was the only word that came to mind. I heard Garry give a gasp and his wide open eyes surveyed my body. Although not as slim as I would have liked I must admit I had the shape that caught the eye and the imagination. My hips have been described as good child bearing hips. This description has usually been applied by men who have gripped them while fucking me from behind. And my tits were a reasonably firm forty two inch double D. so certainly more than a handful for anyone. In fact I stood in front of Garry and caressed them slowly and pushing them up and outwards. This I find always seems to stimulate men; it has always been a sort of enigma as to why men like huge tits and enjoy seeing women caress them. I suppose a lot of psychiatrists have made a lot of money trying to answer that question. Still it turned them on and that is the main thing, and I stood there for a few tantalising seconds fondling my breasts and generally stroking my body. While lifting up and kissing one of my tits I let my other hand slide down my body and my middle finger gently and tantalisingly slid between my legs. Another thing I have learnt is that men like to see women stimulating themselves and Garry certainly enjoyed the show.

Anyway back to work. I picked up the new bottle of oil and returned to the patient.

'Absolutely gorgeous tits Liz.'

'Thank you. These have got to come off' I said pulling at the waist band of his shorts.

He just lifted his pelvis slightly from the bench and I slid them off. Now he was as naked as I was. I poured another pool of oil onto my palms and massaged it into the small of his back. Then slowly and gradually rubbed it into his buttocks which were just as muscular as the rest of his body and I felt them tense up.

'Relax.' I said in my most seductive voice.

He gave a sigh and I could feel the tension dissolve. I leaned over and let my tits dangle over his bottom and let my proud erect nipples run backwards and forwards between his buttocks. Garry raised his head and looked. All he could manage was 'Oh God' before he lay down moaning gently with delight. I rubbed oil into the backs of his thighs then pushing both hands between them I urged him to open his legs a little. My hand just touched his balls and he gave a little whimper. My fingers trailed back up his crutch and between his buttocks. With more oil on my fingers I ran them between his buttocks again this time pressing down so that they went deeply between his cheeks passing over his arse hole. This made him shudder visibly.

'Don't you like it?' I questioned.

'Oh yes I love it. Donna would never do anything like that though.'

I let my finger play around his hole then gradually worked it inside him just a little.

'More?'

'Oh yes.'

I gradually worked my finger in until it was up to the knuckle and would go no further. I waggled my finger about inside him as he groaned in ecstasy. I think he would have let me do this all afternoon but my finger was beginning to ache and I was anxious to see what he had on the other side.

'Right, done that side. Turn over I commanded.'

He did so and his cock twanged to attention. He was really ready for relief and his bell end was glistening. I took hold of it and rubbed his moist end around each of my tits.

'Make me come.' He begged.

And I took his cock in my mouth. My head went up and down slowly as I took in as much of his shaft as I could. On and on I went and I could feel that tell tale rippling within his cock.

'Oh Liz I'm coming' He moaned 'Let me come over your tits.'

I continued working him with my hand rubbing up and down his great length and letting my tits rub across his throbbing cock.

'Faster' He begged.

But I was in command and I knew if I kept a slower pace his orgasm would be greater. I did not have to wait long and his bell end was like a volcano and his come shot out between the valley of my tits. I could see the rest of his come pulsating out of his knob end and over the back of my hand. Garry was relieved and his stiffness a fading memory.

He staggered back into the changing room having decided to forgo the rigours of the gym and I took his place on the couch. As I lay there with the soles of my feet together I put my sticky fingers to work satisfying myself. My pussy was juicy and my clitoris needed my attention. I worked it as only I know how and thinking of Garry's erupting cock, I erupted into orgasmic rapture myself.

Ah, the memories linger on, and as I stood on the balcony I came back to reality. The chanting fans were now leaving the ground and I could hear the stampede of eager feet tramping along the corridor. My afternoon session was arriving.

Derek the captain was the first to enter and he made the rest wait outside the door.
'Are we still on for a promise.' He enquired
'Of course, in fact I've been looking forward to it all day'
I was looking forward to it and I was ready. I had spread thick mats out on the gym floor and I moved over and stood in the middle of them. I unzipped the front of my dress and let it drop to the floor and kicked it away followed by my shoes. I was naked and ready. Derek stood opened mouthed like Garry had done before, at the sight of my tits. Then almost as an afterthought he whipped off his strip. He was sweaty and had streaks of mud on his thighs but what the heck, this was going to be sex at its most raw. He launched himself at me grasping and stroking my tits. He did kiss me briefly then his mouth went to work on my nipples. He fell to his knees and buried his face in my cleavage kissing and sucking like a man possessed. Pulling my waist I knew he could not wait so I sank to my knees and lay on the floor with my legs open. He stared longingly at my pussy.
'Well, don't just look at it, fuck it.'
And he dived on me and I felt his cock thrusting deeply inside me. Derek played his sex like his football, roughly, and it was soon over, but I didn't mind as there were ten more cocks to go. The next two were very similar and were soon over. Number four, Dave had a bit more finesse

and would have licked my clitoris if he had been the first one. But having said that he was good and considerate. He lay on the floor and I got on top of him and I was in control. I could feel his cock deep inside as I jockeyed backward and forward rubbing my clitoris along his pelvis. He held himself back remarkably well and I could feel the grip of pleasure taking over me. Faster and faster I went my tits were shaking and it suddenly burst forth and I screamed out 'I'm coming' and my body was consumed with the ultimate pleasure. This was brilliant and Dave still hadn't come.

The others were getting anxious and had obviously been watching. The next thing was that Simon had come for his action and was standing astride Dave with his prick before me. I took it in my mouth and sucked him off while still gyrating my cunt around Dave's cock. It wasn't long before both of them came at the same time. Derek sending strands of hot come into my cunt and Simon filling my mouth with his.

Two others had joined us aching for pleasure and they stood either side and just jerked themselves off over me. One came over my tits and the other down the side of my face and neck.

Geoff wanted me on my back and he lifted my legs high and wide and in a kneeling position he thrust long and deeply. And again we were joined by two more who just stood either side and jerked themselves off over me.

Eventually they were all done and gone. I lay on the carpet thinking what a fantastic experience this had been. My face, tits, in fact all my body was covered in mud and come cream. I stood up and felt it running down my thighs. I'll join the boys in the shower I thought. I reached a towel off the dance rail and looked at myself in the floor length mirror. I had never seen so much come before. Wiping most of it off I heard someone come in.

'Oh sorry' said the timid little voice.

It was Russ the janitor. He was a short, spectacled, shy man and had been with the club for a couple of seasons.

'It's alright Russ come in.' He had obviously not heard about the orgy and had come in to put away some equipment. His glasses were beginning to steam up as he drooled over my huge tits.

'I, I, I,' he stammered.

'That's OK Russ, relax' I felt slightly sorry for him and wondered what sort of equipment was contained within his boiler suit. I pulled him towards my naked body and removed his steamed up glasses and put them in his boiler suit pocket. He was not bad looking really and I unbuttoned his boiler suit and he was only wearing boxer shorts underneath. Taking his boots and socks off he removed his boiler suit. He stood there in his pants looking very shy and I realized that I would have to take the initiative. Pulling him towards me I realised how short he was because he was at a convenient tit height and he went at them like an animal sucking and nibbling ferociously. Even after all that sex I was getting steam up and I wanted more and I hoped Russ could fulfil his obligations.

I wanted to see his equipment so I kneeled down and started to pull down his pants. I could see from the bulge that he was quite well endowed but when his pants dropped I got the surprise of my life. His cock was huge, absolutely monstrous. Without a word of a lie it must have been between ten and twelve inches long and so thick I could not close my hand around it. God I wanted more of this. I tried to suck him but I literally could not get his cock in my mouth, his bell end was too big. Feeling slightly nervous for the first time I lay on my back with my legs open. 'Fuck me Russ' I whispered and he too like Geoff earlier took my ankles and lifted my legs high and wide. I reached between my legs and guided this giant cock towards my pussy. Would it go in I questioned myself. I need not have worried. Although an incredible tight fit that stretched me to the limit, it did go in. I could not take the whole length but it was an incredible feeling having a cock like this rammed inside you. As I lay there I could see our reflection in the mirror and it was a sight to see that huge cock thrusting inside my cunt and being so thick and stretching me it rubbed my clitoris on each thrust and it was not long before once again I could feel the grip of orgasm welling up inside me and I cried with pleasure as I came. Almost simultaneously Russ came and I felt the gush of his come fill my cunt and in the mirror I could see his massive dripping cock fucking me almost unconscious.

This was the best part of the best day of my life and in time to come I was to re-enact it many times.

GONE CAMPING

Dale and I were on holiday at last. We could put our mundane boring jobs behind us for two weeks and look forward to freedom and sexual bliss. The weather was good and the forecast was for more of the same. We were off camping and I couldn't wait for it, and I mean that in every sense of the word.

Dale loaded the car with all the essentials and we set off. It wasn't an official camp sight we were off to but somewhere off the beaten track, somewhere special that we had discovered. A beautiful place that no one knew about, so no one went there. With the exception of possibly a passing safari, we knew we would be alone.

We drove to a small B&B to leave the car. It was from here that we first discovered our secret place and we had an agreement with the lady who owned it. She would keep an eye on the car for a small fee and if the weather turned sour we would simply stay with her until conditions improved. But I had a feeling this time that the weather would be perfect.

We locked the car, bade her farewell and strode out into the big country. It wasn't long before civilisation was well behind us. No sound of industry, no roar and hum of traffic, just silence and the sound of nature, the singing of the birds, the buzzing of the bees and the swish of the grass as the wind gently whispered through it. The sun shone down through a perfect blue sky, dotted with fluffy cotton woolly clouds. Nature at its most benevolent. Greenery in every direction, I felt free and liberated.

We stopped and held hands. Dale kissed me gently.
'I love you Ruth.' He said meaningfully.
'And I love you too sweetheart.'
'Let's be natural.' He said with a gleam in his eye.
And so we did. We both stripped off completely except for our boots and continued our journey as naked as nature intended. It was wonderful, it was exciting. The feeling of freedom was intoxicating. Not a soul for

miles around, just our naked bodies exposed to nature. The sun felt good on our skin, I could feel its warm glow on my breasts as they swung free as we walked. I could see out of the corner of my eye that Dale was watching them so I stuck my chest out further to tease him.

'Stop.' He said suddenly.

'What is it?' I asked, thinking he had seen someone.

'Go over there to that bush.'

I was puzzled but obeyed his request. The bush was some seventy or so metres away and I walked through the tall grass towards it still somewhat puzzled as to his reasoning. I could feel the grass caressing my legs and thighs as I walked and even felt it gently tickling my labia. I arrived at the bush and stopped and turned to face Dale. He opened his arms and I started to run back to him and at the same time he started to run to me. In my minds eye we were running in slow motion and I realised why he wanted to do it. It was because he wanted to see my tits bounce and swing about as I ran, so I ran to exaggerate their movement. At the same time Dale was becoming aroused and as he ran his cock and scrotum swung from side to side. His cock was getting larger with every swing and his bell end was emerging from his foreskin and I knew what was soon to happen. We met and we pirouetted arm in arm and kissing passionately. I slid from his arms and knelt at his feet. His cock now fully erect and ready for action. Holding it in my tiny hands I could feel the blood pulsating through his veins.

'Suck me off.' He sighed.

And this I willingly did. I gently took his knob end into my mouth and gently sucked it, teasing him gently by licking his end which was now beginning to gently ooze a little bit of come. It was tantalisingly salty as I squeezed his shaft to make it come out. I continued to suck his end gently and I could feel him getting harder and I could feel his pulse on my lips.

'More' He begged.

'In a while cowboy' I teasingly replied.

I could hear him moaning with pleasure and I felt his fingers running through my hair. The time was right and I took hold of his hips and pulled him to me, and looking down I could see the length of his shaft sliding into my mouth. He groaned loudly as his length slid inside me. I withdrew slowly and he moaned louder. My lips sucked his bell end then travelled the length of his cock again until I reached his pubes. I could tell by his groaning and the tension in his cock that he would not last long.

I continued with my thrusting getting ever faster. I gripped his hips pulling myself hard onto him taking his whole length into my eager mouth. I could tell he was about to come and I sucked him faster and faster. He gripped the back of my head and forced his shaft into me harder and harder and let out a terrific roar and I felt his knob end swell and pulsate as I felt his jets of come shoot into my mouth and down my throat. I continued to thrust and suck him as his orgasm died away and I sucked him dry.

He stood there gasping and almost crying with pleasure as he looked down at me and said. 'Your turn.'
I knew what he meant and I instinctively lay back on the grass as it gently swayed in the breeze. I opened my legs wide and gripped the backs of my knees pulling them even wider and at the same time making my cunt available to Dale. He lay down in the grass with his face between my legs and wasted no time in getting to work on me. I felt him kiss my pussy, and then his tongue slid between my lips and into my cunt. I felt him poking me gently his tongue pushing inside my soaking love tube. It felt wonderful and exhilarating and I wanted more. Then he started to slowly lick my clitoris and this is what I really wanted. I pulled my legs further apart and as high as I could so he could really get at me. It was beautiful and I could feel the tension building and I knew I would not be long. He continued to lick me slowly and I mentally willed him on to go faster. 'More, you bastard, lick me harder and faster' I blurted. He took the hint and really slavered over my aching cunt.

Within a few seconds I was coming, the feeling griped me and it shot to an enormous peak as I screamed out 'Oh god' at the top of my voice. I was coming like a volcano and Dale continued licking me even as I was coming down. He really was good and he always delivered. And he also knew that after I had come I still wanted a bit more.

We gathered our rucksacks together and used them as pillows and we fell into a lovers sleep.

I awoke before Dale and as usual I was amazed to see he had an erection even though still asleep. I remember Mum talking to Auntie Flo many years ago about this phenomenon.

'Apparently its quite normal said Flo.' With authority. 'Probably nature's way to stop them rolling out of bed.'

Anyway it fascinated me and I took it in my hand and rubbed it up and down to see if I could make Dale come in his sleep. But with a yawn and a stretch Dale just said. 'Nice.'

I got up, grabbed my rucksack and girlishly skipped off. Dale was up and after me. Out of the meadow we came upon a tranquil river, fed by a waterfall. What an idyllic haven. I stood admiring the scene and Dale and his still erect penis joined me. We instinctively dropped our rucksacks and hand in hand both waded into the water. It was chest high in the middle and although cool it wasn't cold, in fact it was quite invigorating and Dale took me in his arms and kissed me with real meaning. For the second time that afternoon we felt the surge of sexual desires that needed reliving. The water supporting my weight, I wrapped my legs around Dale. I felt his shaft nuzzling against my lips. He took hold of my hips and I reached down and guided his shaft into me. He gripped my hips and fucked me, thrusting me hard onto his cock. I was so light in the water he could fuck me like a rag doll. It was brilliant. I held onto his neck effortlessly with one hand and with the other I could reach down and stimulate myself by rubbing my clitoris with my finger. This always turned Dale on, he loved to see me fingering myself and it made him fuck me harder. The situation was so unusual and erotic that we both exploded into orgasm at the same time and I felt his hot come shoot inside me as my cunt sucked his pulsating cock. He held me tightly in the water then started to wade out. As we reached the bank his shaft was still inside me and as I unwrapped my legs and he lowered me to the ground, it reluctantly slid from me.

We dried and dressed, put up the tent and had supper and a bottle of wine. What a great start to the holiday.

IN PRAISE OF PLAIN

My Dearest Sarah

How I do miss you and how much I want to be always with you. I know you find it difficult to let yourself go and display your feelings. You tell me you feel insecure and see yourself as plain and dull and old fashioned

Oh my dear you are not plain by any means. I see beyond what others see, I see the real woman within. You wear your hair gathered in a bun, you wear large loose and thick sweaters, calf length pleated skirts and large clumpy shoes, your face adorned by the minimum of make up and the largest of glasses. Maybe most men would not look at you twice, but I am not most men, I see beyond the sartorial façade. I see the woman within.

That shy reserved person harbours passion beneath. Passion that is as hot as any temptress. Those glasses cover eyes that exude love and affection, a tunnel to the very soul of you. I can see this. There is no need to be reserved for I see beauty within.

I remember the night before our last parting, we sat together on your settee and I held your hand. I was nervous and I could feel myself shaking, but I must do it I told myself. We looked into each others eyes and we knew. Your lips were so soft and warm when I gently kissed you. My arm moved around your shoulder and I pulled you closer, taking your chin in my hand and gently opening your mouth as it made full contact with mine. It seemed like an electric charge was passing between us. You took off your glasses to reveal the simple beauty of your face, a beauty I knew was there. We kissed again and I held you tighter and I could feel your passion, it was in motion now and could not, would not be stopped. I wanted you Sarah; I wanted you so much it hurt.

My hand slid around your back and I took your breast. I fondled it with such hunger and desire; it felt firm and full beneath your thick woollen sweater. My juice was rising and I wanted you with such urgency, I wanted to make love with you, whatever the consequences. I could feel your hot little body and I knew it wanted fulfilment and you will have it my dear. I stood up and took your hands pulling you towards me and to kiss you again, clutching your bottom and pulling you onto my hard erection. Your hand slid down and rubbed its length urging it on to greater stiffness.

You took my hands this time and silently led me up the stairs to your bed. Unbuttoning my shirt and caressing my chest as you rolled it from my shoulders. I undid my belt and you stopped me so that you could unwrap me yourself, my trousers falling to the floor. Elegant fingers slid into the back of my shorts and gently teased them from me as you watched my stiff manhood twang to attention from the waistband. I kicked off my shoes and socks and stood naked.

Standing back from me you lifted your sweater over your head and released your skirt and shoes. Bra unclipped you let it fall slowly to the floor. Releasing your hair and shaking your head your magnificent breasts shake from side to side relishing their freedom. Just your knickers now stand as a barrier between us and with a naughty glint in your eye you slide them down your lovely thighs. All that is left is your thigh length black thick stockings and you put your foot on the bed to remove them.
'Stop' I say. 'Leave them on, they look wantonly erotic.
You smile a knowing smile. I stand and take in your incredible hour glass figure with beautiful long dark hair. You look a different woman than you did fifteen minutes ago.

We lie on the bed and kiss and caress each other. Taking your breast again I kiss and suck your nipples making you gasp with delight. I must explore your pleasure further and my hand travels down and between your thighs and you purr with pleasure as my finger finds your point of most pleasure. Ever so gently my finger tip teases it, whipping you into a whirlpool of pleasure.
'It's too nice.' You say and push my hand away. 'I want to be fucked.' And you straddle my hips in a kneeling position and guide my manhood inside your cunt.

I can feel my shaft inside you, right inside you as you ride me. Faster and faster you go and at the same time you finger fuck your clitoris. It is a wonderful sight and your breasts shake with your every thrust. I can feel you coming and I can feel myself coming. You tighten around my cock and you cry out uncontrollably. 'Oh Simon I'm coming.'

Your mighty breasts shaking and banging together. It's too much I can feel myself coming, feel myself filling your cunt with my come. Feeling you sucking it out of me.

Oh Sarah it was incredible, you are incredible. You are far from plain my love, you are a Siren of the highest order and I can't wait until I can come home to see you again. Until that time my dear, I love you.

Simon.
X

MY POLYCARBONATE LOVER

I keep my lover in a drawer
A free gift from a ladies night
What a bore
I'm three score years and ten
Not bad for my age I have to say
Still want a bit of nooky now and then
I see you pass from my window
Your body so lithe and desirable
But all I have is my plastic friend
It's big and bold and stretches me which way
Oh to have the real thing this size
So warm so firm and yet so tender
To feel it pulse like a plastic pulse cannot
To fill me full of hot liquid passion
Which plastic has not got
I may be of advancing years
And past the first flush of youth
But I still have womanly desires
And the parts of me that matter still work
And want fucking
If that's not too uncouth

TEA IN BED

It was a beautiful sunny morning when I awoke; a gentle breeze was rippling the curtains, the dappled sun beams dancing on the carpet. Outside could be heard the birds singing merrily and the rattle of bottles as the milkman was doing his rounds. All was well with the world, John had moved up the promotion ladder to a very lucrative position and this was our fifth wedding anniversary. Our financial situation was stable and we had decided that the time was now right for a baby. The pill was in the bin and we were letting nature take its course. It's a fascinating feeling having sex knowing you might, or should I say hoping to become pregnant, it almost raises the sensuality to a new height of pleasure. Yes a child would definitely make our life complete and I was certainly looking forward to the whole process of making that outcome possible. It was even making me feel very juicy just thinking about it, it was Saturday morning, the whole weekend lay ahead to be filled with pregnancy producing sex. How many times could we do it I wondered, or if indeed more was better, or would quantity reduce quality? Maybe a dramatic build up to one fantastic fuck would be best, John's fully charged semen being shot right to the target. But I'm being too dramatic; everyone says you should just relax. People, healthy people have tried and got very upset because of lack of success due to the sheer fact that they have been trying to hard. The sheer tension of fantastic desire has somehow prevented the beautiful event from happening. So that's it, just take it easy, don't try too hard, just relax and enjoy. And enjoy, being the operative word. In the eight years I had known John we have had a good sexual relationship, in fact thinking back we have had some absolutely electric sessions. I sighed with pleasure as I thought of some of them.

I could hear John slowly coming up the stairs with the tea tray gently rattling. This tea in bed ritual was one of the wonders of married life, the little things that give pleasure. No doubt we will still be doing this into middle age when our little brood, when they assuredly arrive, have flown the nest and gone out into the big world themselves, probably having tea delivered in bed and considering the great adventure of parenthood themselves. John entered the bedroom stark naked, except for his slippers, carrying the tea tray.

'Good morning my lovely and happy anniversary. Have you slept well?' He said with glowing gentility.

'Splendidly, and happy anniversary to you too.' I replied blowing a kiss.

I watched his naked virile body glide into the room balancing his tea tray. His penis looked good and alluring even when it was on the slack (if you'll pardon the expression). As he stepped out his thigh would move his scrotum to the opposite side and with the next step it would be pushed back by the other thigh, his penis, large but soft would dangle about provocatively. I watched this spectacle with satisfaction as he transported the tray to my bedside table, his sexual equipment going from side to side and shaking about. John was unaware of my lustful leering as he was concentrating on the over full tea cups. He gently lowered the tray and as he did so I was able to have a closer look as he leaned forward, his penis hanging down for my inspection. The end was just peeping from the cover of his foreskin and I could see the outline of the edge of his glans, this part of his penis had always fascinated me. When he was fully erect and his foreskin had unveiled his splendour it was the part of him I most wanted, this huge bulbous end with this clearly defined ridge. It made my lips quiver just thinking about it inside me, rubbing my G-spot. It dangled about for my gratification as he arranged the tea and biscuit dish. Before me his mighty penis, the phallus that was to inseminate and impregnate me.

I threw back the bed sheets to reveal my naked body to him opening my legs seductively for his delight.

'Well that's a sight for sore eyes.'

'And it's yours for the taking' I replied.

I stood up and threw my arms around his shoulders giving him a long passionate kiss.

'Love you hugely.' I said as I let my hands slide down his muscular chest and sitting on the bed. I took his penis on the palm of my left hand and with the other I gently peeled back his foreskin revealing his bulbous glans. His soft penis was already beginning to firm up with sexual excitement and it had always fascinated me to watch the transformation from soft flesh that wriggled as he walked to huge, stiff, rock hard, ram rod. I took this rapidly firming soft sausage in my mouth and flicked it around with my tongue. I could feel it expanding and growing in length within my mouth and within a very short time it was up to full length and far too big for me to take. Rocking back and forth I let my lips slide the length of his hard cock. (When you get to this level of arousal the vocabulary changes and a penis becomes a cock.) Judging by his moans of delight John was enjoying this immensely.

'Oh Julie.' he moaned let me come in your mouth.'

Normally I would have obliged but this time I wanted him to shoot his come into some other lips.

He held my head and was urging me down harder on his cock; he was getting close to coming so a change of position was called for. With one final suck I pulled back from him and his cock came out of my mouth with a twang.

'It's my turn now.' I said girlishly and moved into the middle of the bed. I opened my legs as wide as I could, holding my thighs just below the back of my knees pulling them wide open so that my lips parted and my cunt was pointing up and easily got at.

'Lick me, suck me, and then fuck me.' I demanded.

John lay on the bed and buried his face between my legs. I could feel his hands under my buttocks lifting me slightly and burying his hungry tongue into my hungry lusting cunt. He pushed his tongue right inside me; it was quite incredible how far he could get it up. The sound of his tonguing was truly erotic as he slavered and sucked my love juice. He then changed his tack and started to slowly run his tongue between my quivering lips taking me to new heights of ecstasy. I moaned as he stopped just short of my clitoris. I mentally urged him to go that fraction further, but like me he was the master of the tease and he tormented me cruelly. Eventually he showed mercy and slowly he let his tongue drape over my clit. I moaned with relief. Then he slowly let his tongue pass down between my lips again the slowly back to my clit.

'More, I need more' I begged.

He gave my clit the full attention of his tongue and the pleasure just washed over me, I was out of control and at his mercy, and he showed none. On and on he licked and I was overwhelmed to the exclusion of all else. Soon the inevitable was about to happen, that incredible eruption of rapture was on its way and could not be stopped. It gripped me and took over. It built up to an almost frightening ferocity. It went up and up and up, and then at its peak, I literally exploded into orgasm. John licked on and on.

'More God more.' I begged almost crying with desperation. John did not let me down and my orgasm went on and on. He seemed to sense my plateau and changed his licking to sucking my clitoris and this seemed to make me rise up to a climax once again. It was unbelievable.

I wanted his cock inside me now.

'Fuck me John.' And with one smooth movement I could feel his glans at the entrance of my womanhood. He poised it just inside my lips and when he had positioned his knees to full effect, he stabbed it into me, thrusting it well inside my cunt making me shriek with a mixture of pleasure and pain. It was incredible, that bulbous ridge rousing my insides.

'Fuck me. Fuck me like there is no tomorrow.' I urged.

He fucked me like a man possessed, harder and order, I could feel his shaft slamming into me. My cunt was glowing as his massive cock pumped inside me. On and on he went and I could feel my tits shaking as he thrust me relentlessly.

Eventually he too reached his peak and I felt his cock ripple and pulsate inside me as his semen shot inside my cunt and washed around my cervix screaming out as he did so. As he continued to thrust my cunt tightened around his cock to suck out every last drop of his come into me. If pleasure was a guide to pregnancy I would be expecting triplets now. I held John to me and kept the position for as long as possible to let John's love juice soak into me.

'I think the tea has gone cold.' Said John as I eventually let him withdraw.

'Better go and make some more then.' I replied still holding my legs up.

THE TELEVISION ENGINEER

It had been a long day and as I drove home all I could think of was a long relaxing bath and a quiet evening by the fire. Peter was due back from his business trip in Germany on Friday and it was our eighteenth wedding anniversary the day after. He had been away for nearly two months on this particular project, which wasn't unusual by his standards but I did miss him and the bed is a lonely place when he's not there. For an anniversary present I had bought for him one of those hi-tech TV systems with huge screen and surround sound etc. It was all beyond me, but it was what he wanted and with the football next week he could 'live the game' as he put it. If all had gone according to plan the system should now be installed. I had arranged with Steph next door to let the engineer in and make him tea and be there if he needed anything. As I pulled into the drive I could see the engineer's van, so he obviously hadn't finished yet. Steph appeared at the window then went to the door to let me in.

'Perfect timing. Everything is up and running and the engineer is ready to give you a demonstration.'

'Thanks very much for sitting in Steph, I do appreciate it'

'No problem. In fact it's given me something to do and someone to talk to.'

'Would you like some tea?'

'I won't thanks. Now you're here I'll nip off and catch the shops'

'OK, well thanks once again.'

'Bye.'

'Bye.'

I put my shopping on the kitchen table and went through to the living room.

'Mrs. Walker?'

'Yes.'

'Hello. I'm Andrea. Well it's all up and running, it's just a matter now of giving you a demo of the controls and special features.'

I must admit I was taken aback somewhat. I was expecting some unshaven overweight specimen in scruffy jeans with his buttock cleavage showing. Instead I was presented with a petite attractive twenty five year old with shoulder length blond hair. She was wearing a one piece uniform

55

not unlike the type worn by care workers. It was very tight and figure flattering and it showed off her slim figure to perfection. I had always longed for a figure like that but had given up trying to attain it many years ago. Anyway Peter always said he preferred the 'fuller figure' as he put it, but I think it was his polite way of saying he liked plump women with big breasts. Well, that's what he's got.

'Mrs. Walker. Are you alright?'

'What. Oh sorry, I was miles away. Just thinking about something at work. Sorry, you were saying?'

'The system is up and running and I just need to show you how it works.'

'Oh yes. Of course.'

'Well it's not as complicated as it looks and it is all controlled from this handset. Simply press Menu, then select the...'

She went on with her demo and I must admit it all looked very good and the sound system was excellent, but I have to admit it all washed over me. I could not explain why but I was captivated by this young woman and I felt as though she reminded me of someone from many years ago. Her figure was perfect and I could not take my eyes off her. You could tell by the sheerness of the material that she was not wearing a bra and indeed you could tell that her breasts were so firm that she could manage without one. That theory was also confirmed by the fact that her nipples showed through almost indecently. Her front was also tantalizingly unzipped so when she bent forward to pick up the *Quick Start Guide* I was treated to a wonderful view of her breasts.

'And that basically is it. As I say all the basic instructions I have just outlined are laid out on the Quick Start Guide and for more detailed information there is the main Users Manual. I've left a card with my mobile number on it inside, so if you are really stuck just give me a bell.'

'That's great. Thank you very much. And it's all controlled from that one unit is it?'

'Yes the remote control. Well balanced and laid out in sections.'

She passed the unit to me but my hands were shaking and it began to slip from my fingers. I tried to grapple with it but I felt it going. Quickly Andrea stepped forward and juggling around my hands she managed to catch it in her right hand. Her left hand had missed the unit but had landed firmly on my breast. In the silence she looked at where her hand was, and then looked into my eyes. As she removed her hand she did it in a circular motion as she felt my contours.

'Oh I'm terribly sorry Mrs. Walker' she said with a slight pinkness in her cheeks.

'It's alright, no harm done. Would you like some tea?' I asked hoping she would accept and I could spend a little more time with this delightful creature. She accepted and noticeably relaxed. I think we both felt that there was some chemistry at work between the two of us and I felt both excited and frightened by the thoughts racing through my mind.

She followed me through to the kitchen and I filled the kettle. The shopping was still on the table and she stood transfixed looking at my bag. I looked to see what was taking her attention and it was a cucumber sticking out. I hadn't noticed it in the shop but it had an unusually erotic shape. It was quite bulbous at the end like a huge penis. Andrea removed it from my bag and silently held it upright and close to her. She wrapped her small hand gently around its girth and slid her hand slowly up and down very seductively. Then, while still doing this she gently kissed the end and slowly looked at me with a naughty twinkle in her eye. I had the finger tips of both hands on my mouth and as she continues to kiss this phallus I let my hands slid down my neck and chest and found myself gripping my breasts. Andrea gave a gentle moan and let the phallus slide into her mouth. Her head slowly going down on it and sucking it. It was an unbelievably erotic sight and I could feel myself getting very wet and randy. I was fondling my own tits and I wanted her to do it. She unzipped her uniform down to the navel pulling each side apart to expose the most perfect breasts I have ever seen. Slowly she removed the phallus from her mouth a strand of saliva stretching from it then squeezing her breasts together with her upper arms she rubbed the glistening object between her tits. After watching this I had to think that if it had been real it would have come by now and her tits would have been covered in semen.

Andrea put the cucumber on the table and walked towards me. She took my chin gently in her left hand, pulled my mouth open and kissed me passionately. I embraced her and returned her passion. I could feel her hands sliding up my waist until they reached my breasts. I was overcome with passion and I wanted this women. She was a little shorter than me and she caressed me like only a woman would know how. Then she began kissing and sucking me. She started to unfasten my blouse and because of the buttons being small and fiddly she simply ripped my blouse open and before the buttons had stopped bouncing on the floor she had unclipped the front fastener on my bra and blouse and bra were falling to join the buttons.

She gasped and moaned as she rubbed her mouth over my breasts and nipples.

'Oh God Sarah they are wonderfully huge. They are like melons.'

Not the most flattering description I thought, but they are giving her pleasure and I was enjoying what she was doing.

'Let's go to bed'

She nodded her approval and I took her by the hand and led her to the stairs and she stopped.

'What's wrong?' I said hoping she hadn't had second thought.

'Let me get to the top of the stairs first.'

'OK, but why?'

'I want you to run up after me so I can see your huge titties shaking.'

She got to the top of the stairs and stood to face me. She unzipped her uniform and let it fall to the floor, and then she removed her tiny knickers and tantalizingly threw them towards me. I reciprocated by unzipping my skirt and was about to remove my knickers when she said.

'Stop, leave them on. I want to unwrap the last bit.'

I started to walk the stairs letting my tits shake as she requested.

'Faster' she ordered, 'I want to see those melons really bounce.'

I could not bring myself to run but I did shake my tits and I heard her say 'Wow.' Something else I had noticed was that she had bought the cucumber with her. I took her hand and led her to the bedroom. We embraced and kissed and it wasn't long before she was fondling and sucking my tits again. Then gradually she slid to her knees kissing my belly as she went. Putting her fingers in my waistband she slowly slid my knickers down. It was a wonderful feeling knowing my organ of pleasure was exposed and ready for action. I opened my legs and like a lithe limbo dancer she kneeled between my legs and licked my clitty. It was unbelievably beautiful. She did it just enough to want me to beg for more and tantalisingly she left me gasping and she dived onto the bed giggling.

As she was sitting there she began to kiss and suck the cucumber just as she had done downstairs. My pussy was soaked and I ached to be fucked. She took the phallus from her mouth.

'Watch this' she said.

She lay back and gently pushed it into her pussy. On an on it went and it seemed as though she took an incredible length. When it was obviously at her limit she gave a satisfied moan and then kept pushing it in and out slowly and rhythmically.

I had to join in so I positioned myself in a kneeling position astride her face and leaned over to so I could reach the phallus.

'Oh yes sixty nines.' she said.

She pulled my buttocks down and I spread my legs so that she could lick me. I in turn lowered myself so I could do the same to her. She had the cucumber still inside her so I took it in my hand and continued with the thrusting. There was just enough room to lick her clitoris and this combined with the thrusting phallus sent her into moans of rapture. I also felt her licking me. She was very skilful and I could feel her tongue running the length of my lips until she found my point of most pleasure and being a woman she knew how to play with it.

'Harder' she cried. 'Fuck me harder. Ram it up me till it hurts.'

And I did. I fucked her and licked her as hard as I could and I could feel her licking me and I knew the climax was not far away. I could hear her moaning getting louder but she never stopped licking. We were both going to come at the same time and I licked her faster and fucked her harder. I was coming and I felt her fingers clawing at my buttocks and she came at the same time. We both screamed out pleasure simultaneously. That overwhelming surge, that body gripping pleasure seemed to go on for an age. I could feel the phallus being gripped by her as her cunt rippled and sucked it.

As it died down I slowly pulled the phallus out of her.
'Oh Sarah' she sighed. 'That was better than any cock'
I turned to face her and we kissed and embraced and fell asleep in each others arms.

THE PICNIC

It was a beautiful day in early June, the sun was shining and the sky was filled with pure white cotton woolly clouds. Perfect weather, warm and comfortable. Susan and I were going for a picnic in the country, very Victorian I know but it was what she wanted. We walked hand in hand along the tree lined lane the leaves creating dappled shadows as they swayed in the gentle summer breeze.

'We used to come up here when I was little.' said Susan 'with my sister and two cousins when they came for weekend sleep overs.'

As we walked I felt very lucky to have a girl like Susan. She was very attractive with shoulder length blond hair with a fringe that framed her pretty face. Blue eyed and fair skinned and a figure that could be best described as, just right.

'This way,' she said pulling my hand, 'it's just through the hedge and at the top of the meadow. A bit overgrown now, but look you can still see the hideaway, its still there.' She said enthusiastically, obviously drinking in her memories of yesteryear.

We arrived at the top of the meadow and it was indeed a pleasant place. It was almost like a miniature forest with a carpet of grass and it commanded a breathtaking view of the surrounding countryside. Not a soul could be seen and only the lazy sounds of cows in the distance. An idyllic place indeed and I can understand a group of children having innocent adventures here.

I spread the blanket on the ground and we tucked into our picnic. Susan regaled me with stories of their childhood adventures playing pirates and climbing the trees. Her voice faded into the ether as I sat looking at her beautiful being, knowing I loved her and wanted to be with her forever. We had eaten most of our food and sat sipping our chilled white wine. The whole scenario was perfect. I leaned forward and gently kissed her warm full lips.

'I love you,' I said slowly. She looked at me and smiled.

'I love you to.'

I moved the picnic things to one side and moved closer to her and kissed her again, more passionately this time. She responded by embracing me firmly. As we sat we held each other still kissing and I gently lowered her on to her back. I leaned over her, my kissing becoming more eager and feeling the tide of lust rising within me. I loved this woman and I wanted her. My hand moved up until it found her beautiful young firm breast and I caressed it longingly. I felt her moan as we continued to kiss and I groped her more and more. I was aching for her and eagerly my hand travelled down to her thigh and found the bottom of her dress. I thrust my hand inside her thighs and moved it up. I could feel the smoothness of her nylons until it reached a bare thigh. My heart pounded more and more as I new she was wearing stockings, erotic stockings. On went my hand until I reached her warm crutch. I could tell by the feel that she was wearing substantial underwear. She moaned as I touched her intimately, then gently pushing my hand away, she stood up, unzipped the back of her dress and let it fall to the ground kicking it away casually.

It was indeed a sight to behold. The sun shone though the branches and high lighted her blond hair and delicate features. She wore a black, all in one corselet, which contrasted beautifully with her pale skin and displayed her hourglass figure to perfection. And as I surmised she was wearing self supporting stockings and those few inches of bare thigh is a sight that has beautifully tortured red blooded men ever since they were invented. She moved to pull down her shoulder strap.

'No,' I said, 'don't take it off.'

She looked at me slightly puzzled.

'Just take your knickers off.'

She willingly obliged, she unclipped the bottom of the corselet and slid down her knickers, then the loose parts of the corselet she tucked up inside so the bottom of the garment displayed a straight line like a 1940s style swimming suit. Any one looking at eye level would just see this beautiful creature in erotic underwear, but me sitting on the ground could just see a tantalising glimpse of her womanhood, those erotic folds of flesh which were highlighted by the black material. It was an incredibly erotic feeling knowing that she was almost fully clothed but her cunt was there for the taking.

I stood up and quickly disrobed and within seconds I stood completely naked, displaying my body for her inspection. She eyed me up and down and her eyes fixed on my cock, it was fully erect and it wanted to be inside her. I took her in my arms and we kissed long and passionately all the time my mind was thinking of her beautiful desirable body. The fabric of her garment was smooth and silky and very sexy to the touch. I took her breast again, it was wonderful, and she moaned gently as I fondled her. Slowly I lowered myself to kneel before her letting my hands slide down her smooth encased body. I kissed the bare flesh of her thighs getting gradually higher towards her womanhood. Her hands slowly slid down her front and her fingers gently parted her lips so her clitoris could receive my tongue. I felt it firm and erect as my tongue licked and teased it lovingly. She moaned louder; I had obviously hit the spot.

'I want you, I want you inside me.'

With one final thrust of my tongue I let her go. I lay on my back seeming to know what she wanted. And I was right; she stood astride my hips and gently lowered herself upon me. She held my stiff, throbbing manhood upright and guided it between her wet lips which eagerly awaited it and sliding down the sides of my shaft. Lower and lower she slowly went until her cunt had taken the whole length of my cock. We both moaned with pleasure as we felt my cock reach the furthermost reaches of her cunt. Her hips slowly went up and down and I could see her lips sucking me, and then descending upon me once again. It was an incredibly beautiful and erotic sight.

After a few minutes of this tantalising sex she changed her tactics. She came down upon my length fully and then slid her hips backwards and forwards so that my cock waved to and fro inside her. Her momentum picked up a gear, and it was obviously giving her great pleasure by the amount of moaning she was doing. Faster and faster she went and at times it almost felt as thought she would snap off my cock. She braced herself with her hands on my chest and I could feel her clit rubbing against my pelvis. She went faster and faster in a sexual frenzy.

'Fuck me Susan, fuck me hard.' I pleaded, and this seemed to take her to new heights of passion.

'Oh God.' She screamed and her nails dug into the flesh of my chest.

There is no more erotic sight than that of a woman having an orgasm and I came at the same time filling her hungry sucking cunt with a gush of hot come the likes of which I have never experienced before. It felt as though the torrent wouldn't stop.

Passion sated, we lay arm in arm sipping the rest of the wine. It had been the best fuck of all time and over time I'm sure we would try to better it. I could not get over the pure eroticism of it, I was naked and she was almost fully clothed, just her cunt open to the world, and now it was full of my love juice. This was more than just lust, I really loved Susan.

OH CLAIRE

Oh Claire you are such a sweet thing, so lovely and full of life.
And yet I know you are troubled. But you need not be.
I know what ails you it is your figure so full.
But to me you are perfect in every respect.
I love to hold you and to feel your warm body
To look into your face and see your beautiful smile
Oh Claire its true you are bigger than most
But don't fret that's better by a mile
Your hair frames your pretty face
That enchanting smile that glows and warms the soul
And those eyes that sparkle and speak of love
It does my heart good to see you there naked
So honest and open with that beautiful smile
And I to disrobed you and holding you close
Oh Claire I want you so much
With me you are my everything my friend my partner my lover
That body to me is beautiful your breasts so large and inviting
They give pleasure to the eye and to my being.
I kneel before you for to worship you body
Your breasts like deities that must be worshiped.
I take them in my hands and caress them. I kiss them and suck them.
I almost wish I could eat them. My tongue gently teasing your firm
erect nipples.
My lips sucking them and my teeth gently nibbling them.
Such breasts to crave for. From birth to death I never want to leave
them.
Oh Claire let me make love to your breasts.
As I lie on the bed tantalise my shaft with your breasts
Your beautiful hanging orbs either side of me gently stroking me.
Bringing me to the height of pleasure.
Rhythmic and irresistible your magnificent breasts caress my shaft
Until finally I can hold my passion no longer and I explode with
pleasure.
And gush my pent up longing all over your breasts.

Oh my dear Claire, what can I say.
You now lay beside me still a sparkle in your eye
Your breasts still majestic and anointed with passion.
Now it's your turn to be worshipped and I kiss your tummy and ever
lower
To search out your pleasure

Lower and lower I go until I find your furry mound
Oh Claire opens your legs for me
And with that I lie between your thighs
I have found what I have been seeking and I kiss your sweet lips
You read my mind, as your hands slide down and your fingers part
your glory
There before me is your magnificent womanhood
I run my tongue between your lips first from the top and slowly down
until I reach your tunnel of love
Pushing my tongue inside I hear your little moans of pleasure.
I keep pushing it in and taste your love juice
My tongue explores up between your lips
Licking you up and down until I reach your cherry at the top
It is firm and erect and wants to be sucked
I cannot deny it pleasure and lick it slowly and rhythmically.
I can feel your pleasure I can feel your body coming to orgasm
You cry out "suck me"
And I suck your cherry as your pleasure explodes into a scream.
Both satisfied and arm in arm we fall into a lovers dream.

A NIGHT TO REMEMBER

It was ten o'clock and I was putting out my empty milk bottles. I lived in the upstairs flat of a converted terraced house, one of only a few that had been converted. The street consisted of two rows of old terraced houses, and was dark and silent except for the sound of a pair of stiletto heels approaching. My heart quickened when I realised it was Margaret. Margaret lived on the opposite side of the street several doors down and I have to admit I fancied her enormously. I first noticed her soon after I moved in. I was driving to work one night when I saw her walking with her husband and two daughters. This seemed to be a ritual for them on Monday evenings, and as to where they were going I have no idea. As I drove past Margaret looked at me and our eyes met, or so it seemed, because I think it unlikely that she would have been able to see me in the dark shadow of the car. Anyway eye contact it was, and the look of sadness in those big round eyes was incredible and it stuck in my mind all through my shift. As I say I really fancied her. I was single with no ties but she had a husband and family and they looked good together. What right had I to interfere? That said, as time went by my feelings for Margaret grew stronger. I could not explain why but it was definite, almost reckless desire. She wasn't bad looking, no beauty by any means, just five feet tall with a well rounded figure. Big round eyes in a pleasant round face and hair cut into a round style that complemented her features. She was slightly scruffy, but in a cuddly sort of way.

I had discovered from conversation with neighbours, who on the whole were past retirement age, that she had been given a bad time by her husband the year previous. He had had an affair with someone he worked with and when she found out she took it badly. Hence the mournful eyes that night. The neighbour continued to say that although the affair ended, and he remained with Margaret, she was wounded by the incident, and quite rightly so I thought. He had cut her, he had cut her deep.

Now this beautiful creature was walking down the street, the silence only broken by her footsteps. She had a canvas shoulder bag and walked looking at the pavement.

'Hi' I called out when she was nearly level with me.

'Oh hello.' She replied somewhat surprised as her mind was obviously on other matters

'Err, pleasant evening.' I stammered out stupidly, not being able to think of anything more original.

'Yes, very nice.' She said with a smile that lit up that beautiful captivating face.

'Would you like a coffee?' Why the hell I said that I don't know, it just came out on its own. She hardly knows me; she's not going to accept an inept invitation like that. She looked at her watch.

'OK.' And she walked over.

I could hardly believe it. A woman of whom I had lusted over for months was coming into my flat for coffee.

'I've noticed you walking up and down' I said.

'Yes I've seen you as well. From my bedroom window'

She had seen me from her bedroom window. Had she been watching me as I had been watching her I thought?

'Coffee, or would you like something stronger, I have some cider.'

'Cider, yes lovely.'

My heart pounding I went to the kitchen to pour the drinks.

'So, have you been visiting friends?' I ventured.

'Swimming' she said sipping her cider.

I had only spoken to her on a few occasions but this woman felt right for me. The conversation, such as it was petered out and I found myself just looking into her eyes. I moved my face close to hers and gently kissed her on the lips.

'That's nice' she said and I kissed her again for longer, and I felt her soft hand on my face. I gently took her chin with my hand and pulled her mouth open. Putting my arms around her shoulders and tiny waist I kissed her more passionately my tongue seeking out hers. She was responding and holding me to her tightly. My lust was quickly reaching boiling point and I clutched her ample breast caressing it lovingly. She gave a gentle moan of approval. She excited me immensely and I wanted her there and then. My roaming hand rapidly descended her stomach and crept between her legs and I could feel her warm cunt through her skin tight jeans. She moaned in ecstasy. I could wait no longer. I stood up and whisked off my T-shirt dropped my jeans, kicked off my trainers and slowly, very slowly slid down my shorts. My cock was throbbing hard as it twanged past my waist band. Margaret's big eyes got bigger at the sight of it. My pants fell to the floor and I stood naked except for my white socks which I left in place as I didn't want to risk stumbling taking them off and spoiling the romantic atmosphere. I took my cock in my hand and let it run its length. Margaret's eyes were still glued to it. I held my arms out to her.

'Come to me'

She got up and into my arms. She looked up at me and we kissed. I took her breast again and fondled it with renewed vigour, I could tell she was braless and feeling the firmness of her full breast, she did not need one. Lifting her top up and over her head her lovely tits fell free. I kneeled and unzipped her jeans and peeled them off taking her shoes with them. Just one barrier now lay between us and I eased my fingers into her waist and gently slid down her knickers. Her warm inviting cunt was before me. I kissed it in homage. I stood up and put one arm round her back and the other behind her thighs and lifted her into my arms and carried her through to the bedroom and gently laid her onto the bed.

She lay there demurely, looking at me longingly, her knees raised and she teasingly opened her legs giving me a full view of her magnificent spectacle. Her hands slid down and her fingers gently stroked her juicy lips. Patting the bed by her side I lay beside her. She kissed my chest and licked my nipple as her hand found my eager cock working it magnificently. Her kissing got lower until she reached my manhood and took its full length into her mouth. As she sucked it almost felt as though it was getting bigger in the vacuum of her mouth. Getting up and sitting astride me my cock sank deeply into her hungry cunt and I could still feel her sucking me with different lips this time. She was good, she was very good and she moved her hips back and forth at frightening speed gauging the strokes perfectly so as not to let my cock slip out of her and at the same time getting maximum thrust. She had her left hand on my chest to steady herself and with the middle finger of her right hand she was working her clitoris. It was a magnificent sight made more magnificent by the sight of her beautiful firm tits shaking in unison with her fucking. It wasn't long until she cried out in orgasm and she seemed to suck my cock in further for those last few strokes. She moaned, almost crying with pleasure as her orgasm reached its climax and then levelled out.

'Turn over for me Margaret' I begged.

She kneeled at the edge of the bed and I stood behind her. It was a wondrous sight and her cunt lips were open and waiting for me. They didn't have to wait long and Margaret moaned as my cock entered her cunt again. This was pure wanton lust and I thrust into her as hard as I could. I could see my cock entering her and as I pulled out her moist lips sucked me. On and on I went faster and faster and harder and harder. I could see ourselves in the mirror and Margaret was watching herself being fucked her tits swaying with my thrusting. Eventually it was too much and with a final hard thrust I sent my hot come flooding into her eager, tight, little cunt.

It was beautiful and she was beautiful and I dearly hoped that we would do it again very soon.

SHOWER ROOM

The weather had been kind so far this summer and I took every advantage of it. For most of the afternoon I had been lying naked, soaking up the sun. We were very fortunate living here, we weren't over looked, and farm land stretched to the distance, so it was very private. It gave me a warm glow when I thought of some of the intimate moments Rob and me had enjoyed on this inflatable airbed on the patio. Who knows we might indulge ourselves later, if the fancy takes us.

It was nearly three o'clock; Rob would be home from work soon, so time for tea I thought. I must admit the sun tan was beginning to deepen and looked very good. Catching my reflection in the French windows I noticed I had a bit of a belly developing; time to sign up for a session at the gym I thought. But on the whole I wasn't in bad shape for my age. What am I talking about, *age,* I'm only thirty five. Maybe over the hill for professional sport but I can still fuck like the rest of them. I let my hands caress my tits, lifting them and them letting them drop, not bad I thought they don't wobble all over the place, just one shake and they assume their posture.

Rob loved my tits and he would be like a child playing with them for hours. It gave me a glow in my pussy when I remember the time we sun bathed together. I kneeled I front of him and took his mighty shaft into my mouth and sucked him to ecstasy, well nearly ecstasy, because although if he insisted I would take his come in my mouth, out of choice I would rather not. But what I did do was to suck him till I felt his cock tighten and I knew he was coming then finish him off with my hand and let him shoot his come over my tits. It was quite a thrill and if I had got the rhythm just right it squirted out with quite a force and I could feel his come slap onto my tits and I watched it shower over me and slowly drip down.

That used to really excite me; it gave me a buzz knowing that I had given him sexual ecstasy. Now it was my turn. I lay on the air bed and let him lick me. I can feel his tongue sliding between my lips, teasing my

71

clitoris then sliding down to my love box and pushing his tongue deep inside me. He would do this for a few minutes to get me really excited then he concentrated his tongue solely on my clit, licking it to ecstasy. Round and round and up and down, urging me slowly to orgasm. When it started it was wonderful, the world just disappeared, and there was only this overwhelming feeling of all consuming, body clutching pleasure that took over my whole being. I would grasp Rob's head and force it harder between my legs; this made him lick me with more urgency. My hips would begin to thrust uncontrollably as I tried to force my clitty and indeed my whole cunt into Rob's mouth. 'Suck me' I would beg, clutching his head and forcing my cunt inside his mouth. He obeyed, and I felt my intimate pleasure piece between his lips and I just exploded into unbelievable ecstasy.

Ah, the memories, it made me quite wet just thinking about it. I heard Rob's car pull into the driveway so I just slid into my T-shirt and didn't bother with underwear. It was a long T-shirt so it covered my modesty. I put the air bed in the shower room for the time being. I say shower room; it was actually a wet room. Rob's sister came to stay occasionally and she was wheel chair bound, so it was on the ground floor which made it easier for her. Having said that Rob and I have had some pretty dirty showers together in there.

'Hi' he shouted as the front door closed.

I trotted through and fell into his arms for a loving kiss.

'No knickers,' he said clutching my buttocks and I gave a girlish giggle as he fondled them.

'Like some tea?' I asked.

'I think I'll have a cold beer, then a shower,' he replied.

He took a can from the fridge and took a swig. He kissed me again and I could taste the ice cool beer on his lips. Again he clutched my buttocks and pulled them apart; it was lovely because doing that it pulled my pussy lips open too. Rob stripped naked and stood there with his huge erection throbbing and ready for action. We are going to have sex on the patio I thought and I started to lift my T-shirt.

'No, don't.' He said and taking my hand he led me out.

'I've put the air bed in the wet room.' I said.

'That'll be handy.' He replied, puzzling me somewhat.

All soon became clear. We went into the wet room and Rob turned the power shower on. Instantly my T-shirt was soaked and clinging to me like a second skin. Rob looked at me silent and lustful, then after a pause just said 'Wow.'

I caught my reflection in the full length mirror, my hair tousled and dripping and the wet T-shirt transparent and clinging. My nipples were hugely erect and proudly sticking through the material. It clung to my hips and you could see my pubic mound through it and very gently outlining my moist eager lips. Rob stepped forward an almost reverently peeled of my T-shirt. I shook my hair free and I felt my tits shake slightly.

Rob positioned the air bed under the shower and lay on his back.

'Kneel down and let me lick you.'

I kneeled either side of his head and opened my legs and lowered myself onto his mouth offering my clit to his hungry tongue. At the first stroke of his tongue between my lips I was at his mercy.

'Suck me,' he whispered.

I leaned forward and grasped his throbbing cock teasingly letting my gently clenched fist travel its huge length and girth for a few minutes. Then I took it in my mouth and went to work on him. With my hands each side of his hips my mouth slid up and down his great shaft. I let it go in as far as I dared without choking. It was an incredibly erotic feeling and I could feel his pulse throbbing. At the same time he was working on me and I could feel my cunt swelling as his long tongue slid in and out tantalising me. He then started a rhythm on my clitty; a rhythm I knew would soon reach a climax. My cunt tightened, I knew I was coming; my whole body was shaking with this incredible feeling of ultimate pleasure.

'Oh God Rob, oh God.'

It seemed to spur him on and I could feel his hips thrust urging me to take more of his cock. I felt his shaft convulse in my mouth and I knew the inevitable was on its way. With a cry like a lions roar, his hot come shot like a pulsating fountain into my mouth. I was still coming and this time I took his come and drank in the pleasure. That was incredible and I was shaking with the beauty of it. We lay there on the air bed just letting the warm water wash over us in sheer blissfulness.

DAY IN THE LIFE OF A PLUMBER

I got to work on Wednesday morning after taking two days of my holiday entitlement and had a long weekend of unadulterated debauchery with Cindy. The office was empty, where was Steve? Steve was my boss, it was his business, and we were plumbers. Well he was the plumber really, I was not yet qualified, but I knew nearly as much as him anyway. On the desk I found a note, it read, *When you get in ring my mobile.* It was from Sandra, Steve's wife. Now Sandra was a game girl and she fancied me and I knew if I played my cards right I would be in with a promise. Perhaps this was it; perhaps she missed me being away and needed shagging. I rang the number.

'Hello,' she answered.

'Hi its Rog, I saw your message. What's up?'

'I'm at the hospital. Steve's had an accident. Can you come over?'

'Accident. What's happened?'

'Multiple injuries. I'll explain when you get here.'

So taking the details I shot over to the hospital

The nurse, in figure hugging uniform that showed her every contour directed me to Steve's private room. I looked through the window in the door and the screens were around the bed. This looked serious I thought as I silently crept in. I could hear Steve moaning from behind the screen. My heart sank and thoughts ran through my mind. What could have happened to him, was he at deaths door, would he ever walk again, had he been burnt beyond recognition? All these things ran through my mind. Would, I now be now working for Sandra. Now that was indeed a plus, I could get my leg over her every payday.

Steve's moaning was getting more intense and I was bought back to reality. What would I see behind those screens? I gently crept closer as the moaning got louder and I could not help myself, I was desperate to know. I parted the fabric of the screen slightly and peered in. I got the shock of my life. Steve had both legs in plaster and suspended by pulleys. Both arms were plastered to the shoulder and set raised to shoulder level and bent at the elbow like a couple of crabs claws. His head was bandaged

74

and his face bruised. And his chest was encased in a plaster jacket. Now I have to say that this highly amusing spectacle was not what gave me the shock of my life. What did give me the shock of my life and the cause of the moaning, which was now reaching a crescendo, was the sight of Sandra sucking him off. Immaculate timing on my part as he shot his load into her mouth and she was sucking him dry. I took a silent exit and waited a few minutes before I re-entered.

It reminded me of the office party last Christmas. I say party; it was just the two of us, me and Sandra. She seemed to like blow jobs and insisted on giving me one. I took her blouse and bra off and she rubbed my cock between her huge tits. Then she sucked me and when I shouted 'I'm coming' she wanked me off and I shot all over her tits. She was skilful with her hands, and my come came out with such force that it slapped onto her tits like a great gob of bird shit.

Peering through the window Sandra was removing the screens and wiping the edge of her mouth. I must remember not to let her kiss me, I thought. I knocked and entered showering mock sympathy and trying not to laugh.

'Whatever has happened to you Steve?' I said trying to sound genuinely concerned.

'I went to do a job in those new high rise flats beyond the dual carriageway. The woman let me in and I could tell straight away that she was a nympho. Anyway I was under the sink turning off the stop cock when the silly cow grabbed me by the bollocks. Well the shock made me jump up suddenly and I cracked my head on the bottom of the sink and it knocked me out cold. The next thing I knew I woke up in here encased in plaster.'

I was puzzled. 'Well why are you all plastered up for a bang on the head?'

Steve winced in discomfort.

'The paramedics did it.' Interjected Sandra wiping the corner of her mouth again. 'The lift had broken and they had to take him on a stretcher down the stairs. Thing is they were laughing so much from the story of him banging his head that they dropped him down thirteen flights of concrete stairs. The only blessing was that he was unconscious so was spared the agony.'

It was all I could do to stop myself laughing.

'I didn't finish the job so you will have to go and complete it' said Steve cheerily. 'And don't let her shag you till you've got the money.'

'As if.' I said.

An hour later I was knocking at her door panting, as the lift still hadn't been fixed. She answered dressed only in a bath robe that was open almost to her navel.

'I've come to fix your tap,' I said.

'Come in,' she said seductively. 'It's in the bathroom.'

'What's wrong with it?' I asked as we entered the bathroom.

'It's the hot tap on the sink, it drips and it's very loose and sometimes it comes on by itself.'

'OK, I'll have to turn your water off first,' I said my thought going back to Steve.

'You look a nice boy.'

'Oh thank you.'

'Much nicer than that other chap. He was a bit gruff.'

'Well he has a lot on his plate at the moment.' She was obviously game for it I thought, but there was something else about her, something I couldn't put my finger on. I was about to go and find the stop cock when I felt her hand on my cock.

'What a nice one,' she said, 'it feels like two pounds of sausage.'

This girl doesn't mess about I thought. With that she let her robe fall to the floor and she stood there naked. She had a magnificent body, very athletic.

'Would you like to fuck me, here, now?' She craved.

'You bet,' I said taking my clothes off and standing as naked as she was.

'Then take me now,' she said throwing her arms around me.

I kissed her, I fondled her tits I fingered her pussy, I was aching for it. The disturbing thing was I didn't seem to excite her.

I lifted her lithe body up by her buttocks and sat her in the sink. Lifting her legs up, I shoved my huge cock right up into her soaking wet cunt. I thrust and thrust, it was marvellous. And worryingly she showed no emotion, absolute silence.

'Why don't you moan?' I asked.

'OK.' She replied rather blankly and looking round the room she suddenly said, 'Have you seen the state of the fucking toilet?'

Not quite the sort of moan I had in mind, but still. As I thrust deeply into her cunt I thought I'm not going to last much longer and she still didn't seem to have warmed up yet. I needed something to divert my growing passion. I needed her to bite me or scratch me or something.

'Hurt me,' I said 'hurt me.

She reached from a shelf a bottle of shampoo and squirted it in my eye. It certainly diverted my passion as the shampoo burnt my eyeball.

Eventually she seemed to get into it.

'Get me off.' She whispered.

Oh yes I thought, great, she's coming.

'Get me off.' She repeated and slapped my face.

Action at last. Once more she pleaded and punched me in my eye. Wow, I thought she is one of them girls who likes it rough.

'Get me off'

She was getting really passionate and punched my other eye, followed by more punches, splitting my lip and breaking my nose. This was great stuff and I fucked her harder and was about to come when she let out a huge cry of 'Get me off you bastard' and with one almighty push she sent me reeling into the shower. My hand knocking the control and I was deluged in freezing water which shrank my rampant cock almost immediately. She ran out of the bathroom screaming and I thought that's the strangest fuck I've ever had but at least I've made her come.

Then it all came clear the hot water tap had come on in the sink and she had been sitting in scalding hot water. I followed her into the bedroom where she was rubbing after sun cream onto her arse. She wasn't badly scalded and I put a bag of frozen peas on her sore spot which seemed to sooth her greatly.

She accepted my apology and I arranged to come round again later. When I do I think I'll bring a twenty inch vibrator and my pipe wrench with me just in case

THE DAYS OF EVE

Oh my dearest Eve
We were so young then those many years ago, those carefree years
ago
You were older by a year and more experienced by a lifetime
You showed me the way and what was what
With your guidance I learned a lot
You broke me in and all others I have compared to you
We sat on the sofa and kissed everything seemed to come naturally
And if it didn't you showed me where to go
We kissed so passionately open mouths and everything
I felt your tongue and I gave you mine
I could hear your heavy breathing and your chest swelling out
My hand around your waist was moving up stroking your side until it
found your breast without
What a delight so large and so firm. I could feel your nipple sticking
through your clothes
I desired you; I unbuttoned your blouse my hands trembling with
nerves and desire.
You stood up, unbuttoned your blouse and threw it on the chair
You unclipped your bra and let it fall to the floor your breasts naked
and free
I was transfixed and couldn't move, what a sight to see
Unzipping your skirt it to fell to the floor just your knickers between
you and nudity
I came to you and standing before you I shed all my clothes
I took you in my arms and kissed you and fondled both your young
firm breasts
'Suck my tits,' you commanded and dropping to my knees I obeyed
your command
I sucked them and sucked them and clutching your buttocks my
fingers found the band of your knickers and I pulled them down and you
kicked them off
We sat on the settee and again I fondled your breasts
Taking my hand you moved it slowly down and between your legs

'Finger me gently and slowly'
On and on it went and I got very excited when you pushed my hand
away and said
'I'm ready to be fucked'
You pulled the pouf in front of me
I sat on it and laid my shoulders on the chair
You stood over me lowering yourself down and guiding my throbbing
shaft inside yourself
Moving back and forth your clitoris rubbed my pelvis
Faster and faster you went almost feeling as though my shaft would
come off
'Oh God I'm coming' you cried with ecstasy
Ecstatically you climaxed and I felt myself coming also
'Fill my cunt' cried Eve. 'Fill my cunt'
And I did.

THE BUILDING SOCIETY

I was thirty five years old and life had passed me by. The reason for this was mother. She had been an invalid for many years, not totally incapable you must understand, she could wash herself etc. but I seemed to be emotionally blackmailed into being a skivvy. Anyway, that aside I was now free as she had passed away peacefully in her sleep six months ago. And me being an only son, indeed only child, she had left the house to me plus the bulk of her estate. The last fifteen years had been a social and indeed sexual blank because of mother's demands and histrionic performances if these demands were not fulfilled. She had had a lifetimes practice at these techniques, Dad bearing the brunt of it until his untimely death, after which I filled his role.

Alas my experience, such as it was with the opposite sex only continued until I was twenty, when I took over the task of mother's go for. Since then I have had to rely on a good memory and a good right hand. But I was able to dream and the object of one of my dreams was Alice who worked in the building society.

I called in every month to pay the mortgage which thankfully was due to be completed in a few months. As I stood in the queue I always hoped I would go to Alice's window. Unfortunately that was not always the case, but if I at least got the one either side I could say hello. From the few times she did attend to me I gleaned little snippets of information about her, the most exciting of which was the fact that she was divorced and still available. Another thing about her was that she was considerably older than me, in fact she was sixty. This I know because on a day when I didn't go into the society, I was passing and looking in from the street I saw balloons, bunting and a banner saying 'Happy Birthday Alice.' This fact did not bother me at all and I looked upon Alice as my perfect partner despite the quarter of a century age gap.

This particular Saturday my luck was in and my turn in the queue corresponded with Alice. I had made up my mind that the next time I saw her I would ask her out, and this was going to be that day. As I

81

approached her window my nerves were twanging and I could feel my legs wobbling like jelly.

'Hello,' I croaked as my mouth had dried up.

'Hello,' she replied with a smile.

I remember talking some utter nonsense about the weather or something. My mind knew what to do but my mouth seemed to be still in gear and running away with itself. She concluded the business and handed back my pass book. My heart was pounding. I had got to do it now and I had got to get it right, or I would not be able to show my face in here again. I took a deep breath.

'Alice,' I said in a voice louder than I expected. The room suddenly becoming silent by my sudden outburst.

'Yes,' she said demurely.

'Would you... would you dine out with me tomorrow night?' There I had said it and it seemed everyone present was watching to see what her response was. It seemed ages before she answered and I was in an agony of anticipation. Plus the cashier at the next window gave her a knowing smile. I felt terrible and I could feel my face going red.

'Yes, I'd love to' she replied casually.

The relief was unbelievable and I even heard someone in the queue behind me applaud. I quickly made arrangements with her for time and venue and made a velocitous exit.

Outside in the fresh air I felt incredible. The woman of my dreams was going out with me tomorrow night. I skipped off home to book the restaurant for the appropriate time, hoping and praying that they were not fully booked at that time. Fortunately all was well.

The next night I took a taxi and arrived at the restaurant in plenty of time. I wanted the evening to be perfect so I ensured I got there before Alice so as not to have her waiting for me. I entered and went to the bar to announce myself and ordered a drink then sat down to wait for Alice. She arrived within ten minutes and she took my breath away. She had light brown hair cut in a short modern style with darker highlights framing her pretty face and her glasses with large lenses seemed to complement her features to perfection. Her dark suit and white frilly high necked blouse made her look very regal. The strange thing was I had no idea of her height as I always saw her sitting down, but she looked in proportion. She was a little bit plump but if anything that made her look younger than her actual years. I got up and took her hands and kissed her on the cheek

'You look wonderful Alice.'

'Thank you Michael, you look very smart yourself.'

'What would you like to drink?'

'Tonic water please.'

It was good to see her and felt proud to be in her company.

The evening was a great success and we got on very well. She even said how flattered she was to be asked out by such a young man. I explained to her that to me age meant nothing to me and I asked her out because over the years I felt that the chemistry was there and it was the right thing to do. I am pleased to say that she echoed my feelings almost exactly. The taxi came at eleven and I took Alice home.

She invited me in for a coffee and I paid off the taxi. She lived surprisingly close to where I did. We finished our coffee and it was time to say goodnight.

Standing in front of the fire I took her in my arms and kissed her gently on the lips. She looked very elegant in her dark skirt and white frilly blouse. As we stood arm in arm looking at each other there was magic in our eyes and we kissed again. I felt her holding me tight and I held her more tightly and our kissing became more urgent and passionate. I could feel her breathing deeply and I knew I wanted her. Feelings that for many years had just been fantasies were coming over me and I could feel the unmistakable tingling of an erection beginning. I pulled her closer to me and she moaned gently as she could feel it too. My hand moved from her back to her side and slowly up until I found her breast. It felt very firm, not too large but just enough. I felt slightly unsure. Should I be doing this on our first date I thought?

'I'd better go before we get into trouble,' I stammered.

'Not yet,' she whispered taking my hand and putting it back on her breast.

83

She inflamed me with passion and I wanted her and I fondled her breast with renewed vigour. Pushing my jacket from my shoulders she led me to the settee. We kissed again and I took her breast once more and I kissed her throat and lower and lower until I reached her breast. Sucking and kissing through her blouse. I started to unbutton it and pulled it over her shoulders. I reached around her back and unclipped her bra and gently pulled it away to reveal her breasts. I reverently cupped them in my hands and kissed each one in turn. They were ample, firm and beautiful.

She stood up and took my hands pulling me up, the effort made her breasts go taught, and then began to undo my shirt. I could feel my shaft was rock hard inside my trousers and after discarding my shirt she let her hand follow the contours of my manhood. Unzipping her skirt it fell to the floor and I did the same with my trousers. I let my underwear and socks quickly follow and Alice did the same with her tights and knickers.

So there we were after fifteen years of hoping and drooling the woman of my dreams stood before me naked. I was taken by the hand to the bedroom and there she lay on the bed with her knees bent and her legs provocatively open giving me a full view of her womanhood. It was too much to bear, I wanted her urgently and my shaft was bursting with lust. She opened her legs wider then slid her hands down her tummy to her pussy and pulled her lips apart.

'Take me,' she whispered.

I kneeled between her legs and kissed her moist warm lips supporting her bottom with my hands her love juice tasted wonderful and I wanted to lick her to orgasm. She moaned gently as my tongue found her clitoris and I gave it all the attention it craved for. Gently licking at first in a circular manner then pressing on harder as I felt her becoming more excited. She moaned louder and louder as she started to climax.

'Harder, lick me harder.' She begged as she grasped my head with both hands thrusting her hips up and down and seemingly pushing her clitoris into my mouth.

'Suck me. Oh God suck me please.'

And as I did so she seemed to erupt into ecstasy. Her back arched and she was almost crying with pleasure. It seemed to go on forever and I continued to lick her clitoris with animalistic passion. As she calmed down I felt it was my turn and moving up the bed my hips were within her thighs and my shaft slid into her. The feeling was so overwhelming, my passion was building quickly and very soon I was thrusting hard, slamming my hungry shaft deeply inside her and all my passion was released and I came in an explosively gushing orgasm inside her.

We embraced and fell deeply asleep. Our relationship flourished and despite the huge age gap we married within the year and are still enjoying ourselves to this day.

COOKING CLASS

It was the last night of the course and a year that I found very interesting. Since Linda had left me for someone who could provide her with a more exciting lifestyle I was somewhat at a loss in the evenings. Also man can not live on just baked beans and boil in the bag kippers, so I needed to learn some basic cooking skills. The class was held every Wednesday evening in the kitchen of the village hall. Cooking To Impress, it said in the advert and I was the only man on the course. Mind you there were only four of us in the group, Minnie and Josephine, two elderly sisters who lived in a chocolate box cottage on the edge of the village with four cats and an aged corgi. Then there was Ruth in her early twenties with a lot to say for herself about how she hated working in a factory and had ambitions of going to America and changing the world. Finally there was Sarah the course tutor. The best way to describe Sarah was, stately. She was a good fifteen years older than me, I would guess in her mid fifties. Solidly built but not fat by any means, in fact in her youth I can imagine her having a classical hour glass figure. Nice wide hips and a large bosom, a very large bosom. Short, full fair hair in a round style that framed her very pleasant face. Yes indeed Sarah was a very desirable woman indeed.

Throughout the year we had cooked some very exotic dishes with varying degrees of success, but having said that none of them were actually inedible. Sarah was a very tolerant and understanding teacher and me being a man and not having the culinary experience that my colleagues obviously had, she gave me more personal attention. She would lean on her forearm in front of my bench giving advice on this and that. Inevitable she wore loose and low cut tops and I was treated to a spectacular view down her cleavage whenever she leaned forward. Her huge breasts seemed to be pushed up and forward and her skimpy bras seemed dangerously inadequate for the colossal task they were expected to perform. Sometimes she would make a side on visit and she always rubbed herself against my arm and I wondered if this was intentional. As the course progressed and I watched her giving advice to the other ladies I noticed they didn't get the breast rubbing treatment so I can assume it was intentional. It was very pleasant and being a gentleman and somewhat naive I always moved away but she still persisted.

Anyway it was the last evening and the atmosphere was informal. Sarah was wearing a tight black skirt and white blouse which was very figure hugging and unbuttoned to a provocative level. I was chopping vegetables and reading my recipe at the same time when Sarah crept up on my right side. I felt my elbow touch something soft but firm. It was of course Sarah's bosom.

'Oh sorry,' I stammered, feeling my face colouring.

'That's alright Alan,' she said seductively as she reached in front of me and picked up a carrot disc and popped it in her mouth.

'Err are those about right?' I croaked, feeling my mouth going dry.

'Absolutely perfect. My, what a nice big vegetable you have.' She said while holding my carrot in her fist. Kissing the thick end slowly and gently, and then giving it a teasing little flick with her tongue. Gently placing the vegetable back on the board she rubbed her huge tits against my arm. Not just a casual contact but a repetitive rub. As she stood up her nipples were hard and erect and very clearly seen through her blouse. In fact they were nearly as large as the carrot discs I had just cut. I stood transfixed unable to take my eyes off them. She saw me staring and casually looked down at her tits letting her hands slowly slide down them as if removing imaginary fluff. Her big eyes looked up and met mine.

'They are yours for the taking Alan,' she said in a low sexy voice.

She then kissed the top of her index finger and blew the kiss to me.

I was making a chicken and vegetable pie that evening but after those encounters with Sarah's breasts my concentration had gone and I had forgotten to put the chicken in. My mind wondered about the future. This was the last night what should I do? I wanted to see more of Sarah, shall I enrol again next September? I thought, no you fool, pull yourself together and do something now.

At the end of the evening we all had an informal talk on the value and enjoyment of the course and we were unanimous that it was a great success and made more beneficial by the fact it was a small class. Sarah invited us to a meal at her house the following week, when we could sample her cooking and we all agreed to go. I was especially keen as it would give me another chance to see her and another week to plan my strategy. The other three students bade us goodnight leaving Sarah and me alone.

'Would you give me a hand to move the table back into the main hall,' she asked.

We took an end each and carried it through. The lifting made her breasts taught and her nipples had become erect again and were showing through her tight blouse. We put the table back in its correct position and I could feel my heart pounding. Not because of the effort of lifting the table but because of Sarah. We were alone in the building and rightly or wrongly I wanted her. I new she was married but something told me that I must react tonight or I would not get the opportunity again. I was shaking with nerves and I might get my face slapped, but I am going for it.

She stood at the end of the table and she looked into my eyes. I could feel that she sensed what I was going to do. Her chest was heaving as I approached and it almost seemed as though those magnificent breasts were getting bigger and her nipples more prominent as I got closer. I grasped her shoulders and gently kissed her on the lips. She was silent. I gently held her chin with my left hand and pulled her mouth open and our lips met again. Sliding my arms around her beautiful desirable body I could feel her responding in kind and we kissed passionately in a tight embrace for what seemed like an age. We paused.

'I was beginning to worry that you were not going to do it,' she said quietly.

'I wanted you since I first saw you on that first night,' I replied 'but I was too shy to tell you.'

'That's one of the qualities that I find most appealing about you Alan, your shy vulnerability. So refreshing compared to the arrogance and selfishness exhibited by most men.'

We embraced and kissed again with an even greater passion. It seemed like urges and forces that had been kept bottled up for years, the pressure constantly building were now about to explode forth. My tongue went into her mouth so far I thought I would choke her, and she responded by sucking it with vigour. I wanted her so much and I needed to have her now. My heart was pounding and my blood racing as my hand slid up her side until it reached her mighty breast. It felt wonderful, so large and so firm and her nipple pressed into the palm of my hand. I fell to my knees and grasped both of them sucking her nipples like a mad man. Shaking fingers fumbled with her buttons then she brushed them away and unfastened them in seconds. Pushing the blouse from her shoulders I almost tore it. Reaching round her back I thankfully unclipped her bra easily. Because of its flimsiness and huge size of her breasts it almost catapulted off. And my God, there they were in all their glory, the biggest firmest tits I had ever seen. They seemed even larger in their nakedness than they did covered up. Simple words cannot convey what an incredible sight they were. I just plunged my face between them and lost myself. I fondled, sucked and nibbled them with an unbelievable passion.

I stood up again and kissed her beautiful lips unable to take my hands off her breasts. I was overcome by passion. I stood back from her and I just stripped my clothes off. I had never done this sort of thing before but there again I had never felt like this about a woman before. I was down to my underpants. This is it I thought, the final frontier. I slid them off and stood there in all my glory. My shaft was rock hard like it had never been before. Sarah's eyes bulged. I had never considered myself a stallion by any means but looking down I must admit, I was impressed. It wasn't that big last time. It was throbbing incredibly and my knob end was wildly bulbous and purple. Sarah unzipped her skirt and let it fall away. She kicked off her shoes and finally slid down her knickers. She was naked and her body was beautiful beyond words. We held each other tightly and we kissed once more. I felt her hands on my buttocks pulling me to her, and then she slid her hand round and grasped my throbbing shaft. Suck me I begged and she descended to her knees and took me into her mouth. I looked down and watched her head going backwards and forwards my shaft sliding in and out of her mouth. I was fast approaching the height of passion and I pulled back. She looked up at me.

'I don't want to come until I've given you pleasure first,' I told her.

At the side of the room were rolls of padded mats used by the judo club. I rolled out a couple to make a makeshift bed. We lay down and I took her in my arms and kissed her at the same time again fondling her breasts which I could not get out of my mind. I had to suck them again and as I did so I let my hand discover her other pleasures. My hand slid down her tummy until it found her mound of Venus then my fingers slid between her legs and found her moist warm lips. Sliding my fingers between them she moaned gently when I found her clitoris. I played with it very very gently and I could feel her arousal.

'Oh Alan I want your cock.'

And she got on top of me kneeling either side of my hips. She took my shaft in her hand and guided it into cunt and descended on it with a moan. I felt it go deeply inside her. She gyrated her hips back and forth rubbing her clitty against my pelvis. She did it so hard I was in fear off her snapping it off but she was in ecstasy. Her head was back and she was whimpering with pleasure her gigantic tits shaking up and down with wild abandon. It was a marvellous sight.

'Fuck me Sarah,' I cried. 'Fuck me like there's no tomorrow.'

This seemed to spur her on to a new level of frenzy and it wasn't long before she was on the verge of orgasm.

'Oh God,' she muttered gently. 'Oh God, oh God' A little louder. Until a final crescendo. 'Oh God Alan I'm coming.'

She screamed and then descended into a gentle sob.

'Oh Alan, I've never come like that before. It was beyond words.'

I rolled her over onto her back with my throbbing shaft still inside her. I got into a kneeling position and lifted her legs high and wide, it was now my turn and I fucked her as hard as I could. In that position I could look down and see my shaft going inside her and thrusting into her tight little cunt and as I withdrew I could see her lips sucking my cock. I thrust harder and harder and faster and faster she looked wonderful lying there her giant tits shaking with my rhythm. Soon it was too much and I could feel myself coming and I gushed inside her, filling her cunt with my hot come. It was wonderful, an electric experience the likes of which I had never known before.

We became regular lovers and despite the fifteen year age gap we were deeply in love. She loved her husband too, but in a different way. A tragic car crash had left him an invalid. She wouldn't leave him and I respected that immensely. I never married again and we were able to keep our relationship going and returning to our own beds at night. In some ways the perfect relationship I suppose. At least, one that suited us.

THE SWINGERS

Today was Ken's birthday, his thirty fifth and we had planned something special for him. When I say we, I perhaps should explain that we are members of a swingers group, which in essence to most people is just an excuse for gratuitous sex with different partners. But I say, why do you need an excuse? Maybe in some peoples mind it puts their conscience at ease, because, OK, they are having a lot of fun with someone they are not married to, but there again so are their partners. Each to their own I say, Ken and I do it because we want to. Most weekends we hold our sessions at each others houses and this weekend it is our turn. Usually it is just a day event starting early afternoon and going on till about midnight, usually finishing with a party or barbeque if the weather permits. Occasionally it's an all weekend affair but this is rare and usually at the latest it breaks up mid morning the following day when over intoxicated revellers try to find and gather together their partners they arrived with and their underwear.

There could be any number of people at these events, but the mainstay of the group were just four couples, including Ken and me, and as this was a special day it was by invitation only, as unbeknown to Ken we had planned for his birthday treat the ultimate sexual torture, which made my cunt glow with anticipation every time I thought about it. More about that later, the guests were arriving and Ken and I will receive them and introduce them to you.

Firstly John and Cynthia who, in their fifties were the eldest in the group. Cynthia was actually my Kens favourite, he said she reminded him of Doris Day and I must admit with her blond hair and big bright blue eyes there was indeed a striking resemblance. She had a full figure, not fat by any means, just well rounded with very generous breasts which I have a lot of video footage of Ken taking advantage of. I think its something to do with the mothering instinct. John too, for his age had a good physique, but unfortunately due to an industrial accident some years ago he injured his back and some forms of sexual acrobatics were a bit much for him. Having said that I have witnessed his technique

92

personally and I must say he has always delivered the goods. He was usually the cameraman for our little sessions and also to his credit he had a unique sexual attribute, which I think I will tell you about later as more guests were arriving.

Edgar and Hetty, a beautiful couple from the Caribbean. Both were school teachers, Edgar took sports and it showed. He was very popular amongst the ladies, his lithe black body was a sight to see and his cock was enormous, a good ten inches of black stiff flesh. Hetty taught maths, she had a bubbly character and when she was present you could hear her raucous laughter all over the house. She had her hair straitened and it was just below ear level, cut to curve alluringly around her jaw line, and a fringe that just came over her eyebrows. She was quite plump, with very large breasts and she shaved her pussy, which I have to admit looked cute. Ken also told me that it was a pleasure to fuck her as she was very tight. Maybe that's why she and Edgar came to these parties; perhaps she was too tight for him.

And finally to arrive, Jack and Eileen. Jack, a dear boy and my favourite, six foot tall with blue eyes and shoulder length blond hair. Very athletic, very fit. Not the hugest cock in the business, but for my money the best. I went juicy just from his kiss. Eileen was a dear little thing, she had very long hair down to her neat little bottom which she always wore in a pony tail and a fringe which was down to her eyes and every time she blinked her eyelashes flicked it. Her figure was complemented by her simple white dress which showed off her breasts. She was a very small woman, well under five feet, with an elfin girlish figure. She had had breast implants and although not large they stood very firm and beautiful and even when she was being fucked to the verge of coming they hardly moved, they just gently shimmered.

Introductions out of the way and everyone with a drink it was time to give Ken his birthday surprise, a surprise of which everyone was in on. The women stripped Ken naked and blindfolded him.

'You aren't going to leave me in the street are you Linda?'

'No nothing like that,' I reassured him.

I guided him into our bedroom, which because of its many mirrors and giant bed in the middle of the room, was always the most popular venue for our sex parties. Also unbeknown to Ken I have had a feature installed that he had always wanted. Eileen took down a couple of pictures to reveal two black metal plates bolted to the wall from which dangled a length of chain and thick black leather manacles. We backed Ken to the wall and fastened his wrists into the manacles and removed his blindfold. He looked surprised and pleased with his present. He shook his arms that were suspended slightly above head level. There was no escape as he rattled his chains.

'Let the torture begin,' I proclaimed. With video camera at the ready to record what I was sure to be an interesting evening.

Eileen slipped out of her dress and let it fall. She was completely naked and stood in front of Ken and tantalised him by caressing her breasts and lifting them up and licking her nipples. She pushed them forward and upward towards Ken's mouth. He leaned forward straining at his manacles, but Eileen stayed teasingly just out of his reach, still massaging her small but firm breasts and moaning gently. I could see Ken's cock rising like a drawbridge as it became erect. The beautiful torture was that it was going to stay erect and unsatisfied for some time and there was no way he was going to get relief until we decided otherwise. Still caressing her petite body she almost floated back towards the bed. She lay down very elegantly she was a very sexy and tantalising actress. She lay with her feet towards Ken, she bent her knees and with her legs together she moved them slowly to the left then slowly to the right making her moaning almost purring sexual sound. Then with her bent legs in an upright position she slowly opened her legs so that Ken had a splendid view. He gasped in amazement at the wonderful sight that opened up before him. Still grasping her tits her hands slowly slid down her body her two index fingers going between her legs and holding open her lips revealing her warm moist little cunt. She started to finger herself and it drove Ken wild.

She seemed as though she was almost ready to come when right on cue entered Edgar the Caribbean stallion with his erection full on. Eileen squealed with delight as she saw what was coming and she assumed Edgar's favourite position. She kneeled on the side of the bed so that Ken had a side on view. Edgar guided his huge ten inch cock into Eileen. She yelped as the huge prick sank deeply into her. Ken watched as inch by tight inch it went into Eileen's tight little cunt. He reached her limit; she couldn't take the full length. Edgar started thrusting in and out trying to get an extra inch of his cock inside Eileen. She cried out in pain and pleasure as each thrust seemed to go further inside. They both came together her cunt dripping as Edgar filled it with his hot come.

Edgar left exhausted and I handed the camera to an equally exhausted Eileen. It was to be my performance next and in came Jack completely naked and just as ready as Edgar.

'Please, please release me.' Pleaded Ken from his manacles. 'I can't take any more, I need relief.'

'Not yet birthday boy, you've not suffered enough yet,' said I cruelly.

After watching Edgar's performance through the door Jack was ready to get at it. He took me in his arms and kissed me longingly. I felt his hand moving up my side and taking my breast. He fondled it expertly and then feverishly sucked it. I was eager and ready for it. I could feel my love juice running down my leg. Jack sat me on the edge of the bed and pushed me back and at the same time scooping up my legs and throwing them over his shoulders. Then without pause or ceremony he buried his face in my cunt. I felt his long tongue go deeply inside me. In and out it went driving me into a frenzy of pleasure. I was gasping for it. Then I felt his tongue between my lips edging its way to my clitoris. I moaned loudly as he found my pleasure and he licked me with such ferocity. His tongue was educated and he knew how to use it to maximum effect. This whole situation was so bizarre so sexually charged, that I felt myself coming. I let out a scream of ecstasy has Jacks tongue set my whole being alight. 'Oh god,' I cried as I let myself go. The orgasm seemed to go on and on and Jack carried on licking and saw me through. He sensed the time perfectly and lifting my body he moved me to the middle of the bed and as he got on top of me I felt his cock slide deeply into me. I was still intoxicated with pleasure as jack thrust at me with gusto. It wasn't long before I felt him throbbing inside me followed by a yell as his love cream filled my cunt.

Poor old Ken, he was almost in tears with the frustration, his cock still throbbing and still unsatisfied. Scrambling off the bed I heard him plead in a weak voice.

'Please Linda; put me out of my misery.'

'Not yet my dear.'

Eileen passed the camera to me as she helped her exhausted husband out.

Next on stage, so to speak were Hetty and John. Now personally I think they made a good couple together. They certainly looked good as they sat on the bed together with John's greying but distinguished hair and pale skin. Which contrasted beautifully with Hetty's dark skin and black hair and of course her cute shaved pussy. John was an old romantic and took great care to *court* Hetty in the proper manner. He kissed and hugged for what seemed an age until his hand finally took one of Hetty's huge dark breasts. She was a magnificent figure of a woman with her forty six inch bosom and thighs that looked as though she could easily break any mans back. John continued to knead her huge breast and gently kissed her nipples laying her back on the bed. Then like Eileen earlier she opened her legs towards Ken, but this was for John's benefit as well.

'Finger me,' she quietly whispered to him.

And John did just that. He gently and expertly teased her clitty with his finger. Then he thrust a finger inside her, then two. He found her G-spot which made her moan with pleasure. Then he continued to work on her eager little clitty and slowly but definitely her passion began to rise as she literally screamed with pleasure. John continuing to stimulate her until her orgasm had died away.

'Suck me.' He begged as he stood by the bedside and pulled her hand. She sat on the edge of the bed her legs outside his and she reverently took his white and purple ended cock into her mouth, her full dark lips travelling its length. She could feel every ripple, every vein of his cock as her eager lips travelled back and forth along its long stiff length. She gripped his buttocks as she pulled him inside her mouth. It was not long before I could tell John was about to come.

'Come over her tits John,' I shouted.

At the opportune moment he pulled out of her mouth and continued to work himself with his hand. Simultaneously Hetty lifted up her huge dark tits to receive him. With a groan John exploded into orgasm and his cock seemed to explode as well. As I mentioned earlier John had an incredible sexual attribute and this was it. He produced a huge quantity of come when he ejaculated and it squirted uncontrollably all over Hetty's tits. The amount of come he produced was amazing and it almost covered both her enormous tits. It was an incredible sight and the white of his semen contrasted beautifully with Hetty's dark breasts.

The show almost over the rest of the gang came into the bedroom. We were all satisfied except the birthday boy who was still shackled and torment and still erect and unfulfilled.

'Oh don't torture him any more.' Pleaded Eileen.

And with that Cynthia, his favourite seductively walked towards him, her very large tits swaying from side to side as she did so. She caressed them pointing them towards Ken. She let him have a teasingly short kiss of them. Then she sank to her knees and clasped his cock with her tits. Ken was in a frenzy of excitement his cock almost bursting with desire.

'Happy birthday Ken.' She said.

She then took his throbbing cock between her lips then let his entire length slide into her mouth. She worked him expertly, holding him against the wall by his hips her hungry mouth sliding up and down his shaft. It seemed only a few seconds and he groaned with pent up pleasure as he came in her mouth. Cynthia sucked him off, taking all his come in her mouth and sucking him dry, squeezing his shaft until every last drop was gone

'Whose birthday is it next?' I asked

'Me, me, me.' They all replied.

And all this on video as well.

ODE TO JOY

'Ten minutes to nine everyone. Start winding up, and closing down the computers please.' Announced June the course lecturer.

I was doing a family history course at the local college, Dad had died last year and Mum five years before and I was ashamed to admit that I knew very little about our family history. My knowledge was particularly scant about my Father's side of the family and I have no memory of his parents at all. I know my father was the youngest of a very large family and as his father died in his formative years, so he had no personal memories of him either. He being the only one of the brothers in his family to produce a son, I realised I was the last in the line. As I too produced only a daughter, I was in effect the last to carry the family name. So I am doing now by computerised research, what I should have done years ago by talking to the family. We were not a close knit family and serious talking was not one of my parents strong points, anyway too late for remorse now.

On the plus side, I had a great Aunt on my mother's side who was well into her eighties and was as fit as a flea, both mentally and physically. In fact she still drove, and at our last meeting she was extolling the virtues of her latest car, which was a two litre injection something or other, of which she was bragging about a speeding fine.

'Which I shan't pay again of course,' she announced with a sort of defiant pride.

She was a tough old bird and in keeping with nearly all the women on that side of the family lived long and active lives. Here's hoping that I inherit those genes. Anyway after several meetings and an equal number of bottles of whisky, I gleaned a mine of information from her which gave me a spring board to investigating the family history.

That said back to the college course, of which this was one of many I had done over the years. I was forty years old, divorced, and had probably spent more time at school now than since I left at seventeen. Was it the latent thirst for knowledge, or was it the desire to fill those lonely empty winter evenings after the divorce. Who knows; or cares. I had never really settled with anyone after that unfortunate affair, it certainly knocks a huge hole in your confidence when your wife dumps you for someone else. After the shock, the anger, the questions why, you start to think and analyse. The question why! Was it my fault? Did she leave me because I wasn't up to standard? Was I sexually inadequate in some way? The more you question, the more you think about it, and the more, it seems, you feel it's your fault. Whatever the answer, or reason its history, like what I'm getting involved with now, so push it to the back of your mind and get on with life.

There was however one member of the group of whom I had formed a fond attachment of sorts and that was Joy. She was a widow and at sixty five years old, was a generation my senior. Having said that, there was something about her that attracted me emotionally and sexually. I had not made any serious romantic overtures to her, other than buying her coffee occasionally during the break, but as next week was to be the final class of the course, if I was interested in her I had better make a move soon, in fact tonight.

Everyone began to gather their things and chatter about the progress or not that had been made this evening. I put my folder in my case keeping an eye on Joy so I could time my exit with hers. I followed her out at a respectful distance as she had been collared by Doreen and my immediate plan of engagement was thwarted. However when we got outside the main entrance Doreen dashed off as her husband was waiting in the car. Heart thumping with anticipation I made my move. Catching up with her I made small talk about some nonsense or other until we were level with my car.

'Can I give you a lift home Joy?' I stammered.

'I only live a few streets away Alan,' she replied, which threw me somewhat.

'But it looks like rain,' I said in obvious desperation.

She looked up at the clear, cloudless, star lit sky, then looked into my pleading eyes, smiled beautifully and said 'OK.'

I think I audibly let out my held breath, and with a knowing smile she got into the car as I held the door for her. I nonchalantly raced round

99

to the driver's side, bruising my leg on the bumper on my way past. It obviously shook the car but I was determined to look cool, and then dropped my keys. Retrieving them I fumbled with the lock and mentally swearing to myself. Door open I got in cracking my head on the door pillar.

'Are you alright?' She said with genuine concern.

'Oh yes. It's nothing,' I fibbed.

I started the car and pulled away and stalled it. I stifled once again the incredible urge to swear.

'Sorry. All thumbs tonight.'

She put her warm little hand on my thigh and our eyes met.

'Relax.' She said in such a slow and sensual manner that I could feel the tranquillity flowing from her hand throughout my body.

The three hundred yard drive to her house seemed endless. We pulled up outside and my mind went blank. I had been mentally rehearsing this moment for weeks and my mouth was dry and my head throbbed still from the encounter with the door pillar.

'Hear we are,' I squeaked somewhat unoriginally.

'Would you like to come in for a coffee Alan, and let me have a look at that bump?'

Wouldn't I just, I thought to myself my spirits now lifting.

As we entered the spacious living room I couldn't help but feel like a spotty, clumsy juvenile out on his first date. It worried me and thrilled me in equal measures.

'Sit down and make yourself comfortable. I'll put the kettle on and get something for that bump,' she said dropping her jacket onto an armchair as she disappeared into the kitchen.

I sat down and sighed. Don't blow it I thought to myself, just relax. What an attractive woman she was, I thought to myself, about five foot three, petite curvy body, pleasant almost childlike face, with shortish strait hair cut to contour her head and face. Her fringe cut slightly shorter towards the centre of her forehead to give an almost short page boy style. It was grey, but a streaked, dignified grey. She wore tight figure complimenting jeans and an expensive looking, white close fitting blouse with embroidered lapels. For sixty five she was a damned attractive lady.

'Let me dab this on your head,' she said bustling in with something on a white cloth.

It felt cool and soothing and certainly took the sting out of the bump. As she leaned forward and over me, mopping my forehead, I was privileged to an excellent view down her ample cleavage, and as she attended to my injury I watched her bosom performing its dance within the confines of her blouse. As I noticed her top button was undone I have a suspicion that this display may well have been partly engineered.

We talked and finished our coffee. There was a silence, a silence that said everything. Sitting next to me on the sofa I turned towards her and took her hand and kissed it. She gazed into my eyes and smiled. I moved closer and delicately kissed her lips then held her closely and kissed her longingly. We never spoke, just held each other and gazed into each others eyes. A feeling of 'this is absolutely right.' flowed through me. I kissed her again and I could feel a sense of desire rising within me and I felt that I wanted this woman more than any in the world. It was not just a sexual feeling but a feeling of wanting and being. I began to breathe heavily with lustful cravings. My hand began to slide up her side and I gently took her breast in my cupped hand caressing it like a precious gem. As I massaged her breast with greater force I could feel Joy responding with more passionate kissing and I felt her tongue searching for mine. Our tongues entwined and I could feel her nipple hard and erect beneath her blouse. I continued to fondle her as my lips kissed her throat on their way to her breast. I kissed and sucked her through her blouse making it so wet that it became transparent and I could see her cherry red nipple through her blouse and bra.

She stood up, taking me by the hand and leading me through to the bedroom. The door closed and she leaned seductively against it with her palm pressed against the panels. I slowly undid the buttons of her blouse and I could hear her breathing heavily. Conveniently her bra was a front fastening type and was easily unclipped. I peeled it back and her breasts, with a gentle wobble were free and being worshipped. I gently eased her blouse and bra over her shoulder and placed them on a stool.

101

Joy had demurely covered her breasts with her folded arms, I gently but forcefully took her wrists and held them against the door so I could feast my eyes on the full glory of her very firm and ample breasts. I kissed her again passionately and took both her breasts in my hands, caressing and squeezing them. I fell to my knees to worship them properly, sucking and teasing them and burying my face in their sumptuous fullness.

I was driven by animal pleasure and I wanted more. Still on my knees I unzipped her jeans and slid them down. I took off her shoes and Joy stepped out of them. I got to my feet and removed my shirt and trousers. Followed by my socks and shoes, not an easy task to perform with allure. Just two pieces of underwear stood between us. I put my fingers in my underpants and eased them down and let them fall to the floor. My shaft was now ready for action, stiff and throbbing. Joy eyed me up and down in delight. I kneeled before her once again and took her waistband with my fingers and slowly pulled her knickers down to reveal her full naked magnificence. I stood up to admire her in full. I was overcome with desire and I wanted her then and now. I took her hand and led her to the bed.

'Wait,' she said still holding my hand.

She took a tube of lubricating jelly and squeezed it into my palm.

'Please rub it on yourself, I find myself a bit dry these days. My spirit is willing but the body doesn't always respond.'

She took great delight I think, in watching me rub the gel into my shaft, and I must admit it aroused me further doing it for her. She took another pool of it in her own hand and lay on the bed and started to rub it on herself. It looked very erotic watching her do it and she new I was enjoying it and played on it more and more. She took another squirt and slowly rubbed it between her now glistening lips and around her clitoris that made her moan with delight when she touched it.

'Put some more on your shaft,' she said in a sexy voice.

I did so. Not because I needed it, but because she had pleasure in watching me and it gave me pleasure knowing she was enjoying the sight. She applied some more to herself, pushing it inside this time with two fingers thrusting in and out to her delight. Then more on her lips and clitoris to make sure. Her clitoris was well attended to.

'I'm ready for you now Alan,' she said in an unbelievably sexy voice and holding her legs high and wide.

I did not have to be asked twice and I got onto the bed and found myself kneeling in homage before her again, this time in front of the full display of her womanhood. Her lips were before me and slightly open and waiting. I kept them waiting no longer and entered her. My shaft slid easily inside her. Her warmth and wetness were unbelievable; it was a feeling like nothing else in the world. Joy moaned with delight as the full length of my shaft went deeply inside her. I took her suspended legs and thrust and thrust and thrust. At the same time Joy stimulated her clitoris with her finger giving it full vent and obvious pleasure. I admit also that I got a voyeuristic thrill watching her do it.

I must admit I was pleased with my own performance tonight. Normally with my former wife I would not have lasted this long. But something about Joy gave me inner strength and confidence and I felt I could fuck her all night if necessary. As it happened she was building to an explosive climax and I could feel her coming. This also started me on the course of the inevitable and I could feel me entering the point of no return. We both came simultaneously in a welter of pleasure, screaming as the flood of my semen shot inside Joy's welcoming little cunt.

We had many nights like that in the years to come and despite the age gap we are still together now and perhaps more importantly, are still very much in love.

EROTIC MASSAGE

I was walking up the stairs jut as Alistair was coming out of the shower drying his hair. He certainly was a magnificent specimen of a man and his penis had that charming softness about it as he strolled across the landing, swinging gently as he walked. He stopped and continued to dry himself gently rubbing the towel between his crutch lifting up his sex equipment onto the back of his hand. Even at this stage it hung down a good four inches and his testicles moved about in his scrotum as he towelled them. I watched him in admiration making small talk about some nonsense or other not taking my eyes of him.

'Are you having dirty thoughts,' he barked.

'Not at all,' I replied unconvincingly and feeling my face glow slightly with embarrassment, as I certainly was having dirty thoughts.

He stood to face me and took his penis between his thumb and first finger and slowly like a striptease artist pulled back his foreskin to reveal his bold, purple bulbous glans. The ridge of which stood proud from the rest of his ample shaft. I sighed to myself as I thought of the many times that huge end had slid inside me and tantalised my G-spot.

His penis had now lost its softness and was beginning to firm up, as he too was obviously having dirty thoughts. He throws his towel over the stair rail and held his arms out and I sank into them putting my arms around his athletic body and cupping his hard buttocks in my hands as we kissed. I pulled him towards me, parting his cheeks and feeling his hardening shaft against my tummy. He unzipped the back of my dress and it fell to the floor and with equal deftness he unclipped my bra. Stepping back a little he teased the loose straps from my shoulder to reveal my naked breasts. Looking down I could see my nipples were sticking out proudly, yearning to be sucked and played with. Alistair stood silently gaping at my breasts. Inserting my fingers into my waistband I slowly slid down my knickers. I could see his eyes urging me on but I made him wait. Eventually they dropped to the floor and I was as naked as he, his eyes staring like a child at my pubescent splendour.

We fell arm in arm again just holding each other.

'Would you like a massage?' He said.

'Oh yes,' I pleaded. 'It's been an age since we have done that.

He then gathered me up in his strong muscular arms and carried me through to the bedroom where he reverently laid me on the bed.

'Turn over; I'll do your back first.'

I rolled over into the middle of the bed as Alistair walked round to find the oil. His shaft was now fully erect and stuck out a good eight inches before him like an unadorned flagpole. Gone was the soft penis that swayed gently as he walked, to be replaced by this giant throbbing ramrod.

I held the pillows as he skilfully warmed the Ylang-ylang oil in his hands and gently rubbed it into my shoulders. I relaxed immediately and the scent of the oil bought back many erotic memories. From my shoulders he radiated out to my arms then down my back. It was fantastically relaxing and I just melted into the bed. Round and round gently rubbing and on down to the small of my back. Then charging his hands with oil he set about my bottom, handling my buttocks like a baker kneading dough, pulling them apart as wide as they would go. This was very pleasurable as not only were my buttocks pulled apart but also the lips of my womanhood were also beginning to part. Putting on more oil, his fingers gently slid between my buttocks, sliding to and fro very tantalisingly, further and further. I could feel his index finger had found my hole and very gently and in a circular motion I could feel it gently slide in just a little way.

'Oh Alistair,' I moaned.

'Like it?'

'I don't know,' I moaned. He had never done this to me before and I wasn't sure of myself, but the newness of it did arouse me somewhat.

He gently manipulated his finger within me for a few more seconds then pulled away and continued massaging my buttocks. His fingers ran between my buttocks again and I opened my legs slightly, mentally urging his hands to travel further down between my crutch, but Alistair was going to wait and leave the ultimate erogenous zone until the end. He continued down my thighs, doing each in turn and then down to my legs. He finished this side by giving my feet special attention and it was surprising how sensual foot massage is.

'Turn over,' he said.

I rolled over and Alistair standing one foot on the floor and one knee on the bed was charging his hands with fresh oil. His shaft was still magnificently erect as he resumed his massage. This time he went directly for my breasts, caressing them gently, pushing them up and together. I was becoming sexually aroused and judging by his firmer fondling of my breasts, so was Alistair. He gently manipulated my nipples then leaning over me took them in his mouth and sucked and licked them. I moaned with pleasure as he continued with greater fervour. He quickly did a token massage of my tummy then his eager hands slid down for an even greater trophy.

His hand slid between my legs and I gasped as I felt his fingers slide between my hot moist lips. I wanted him badly; I wanted sex with him badly. His oily fingers found my tunnel of love and three of them slid inside me and gently shook and tantalised me inside. Alistair was raising me to new height of pleasure. His finger found my clitoris and the oil made it feel more sensitive than usual. I could not stand much more of this.

'Fuck me,' I commanded, surprised at my forcefulness as well as my rustic language.

He was as eager for pleasure as me and didn't need asking twice. He kneeled before me taking my ankles and lifted my legs high and wide and in one smooth action I felt his penis enter me. Slowly it found its way and when it was sure of its position he rammed the whole eight inches inside me with great force. I cried out partly in shock but mostly with pleasure. Alistair fucked me hard and strong and I loved it. On and on he went his huge manhood stretching me to the limit.

'Finger your clitty,' demanded Alistair.

The sheer idea was wanton but beautiful. I stimulated my clitoris to the rhythm of Alistair's thrusting. My clitoris still moist with oil was ultra sensitive and I could feel the ultimate pleasure beginning to build. I could hold it no longer and the sheer maximum pleasure just rose up inside me and exploded forth like an atomic bomb.

'Alistair, Oh Alistair,' I screamed.

Alistair also was about to reach his peak. It seemed to arouse him more being able to watch his shaft thrusting inside me and it also stimulated him watching me fingering myself.

'Oh God Carol, I'm coming,' he gasped.

And I felt his shaft tighten and his love juice flood inside my cunt as he climaxed. It was perfectly timed and my orgasm seemed to make his more explosive.

We then lay in quiet contemplation of the beautiful experience we had just created.

ON THE TRAIN

The sun cascaded through the bathroom window as I stepped dripping out of the shower, my naked form glowing with delight. I looked at myself in the full length mirror and felt proud of my body and the effects it could have on people. I can best describe my figure as, eye catching. A lack of modesty maybe, but people who hide themselves away get forgotten. I will not be forgotten. In the mirror I surveyed my equipment, my bust measured an enviable forty two inches. That coupled with a double D, cup size, a twenty three inch waist and thirty six inch hips gives you some idea of my shape. My hair was dark to match my dark mysterious eyes, and cut into an elfin style to complement my elfin figure. Well an elfin figure with huge tits.

Today I thought would be an adventure day. The usual routine is to drive to the railway station, park up and take the train to work. A dull journey to a dull job. A spice up was called for. I dried myself off, my tits shaking as I rubbed them with admiration. Although they were big, they were full and firm and shapely. Walking through to the bedroom it was flooded with sunlight and as I stood by the window admiring myself once again in a mirror. I was aware that someone else was admiring me. Out of the corner of my eye I could see Mr. Johnson walking past, with his wife yammering into his ear as she always did. He had temporary relief from this audible torture as he looked up and saw me caressing my breasts. I turned to face the window, pushing my tits up and out with my hands and blowing the poor man a kiss. Mrs Johnson also noticed my mammorial display and paused long enough in her verbal dysentery to slap him round the back of his head. Poor Mr. Johnson married to that, I'll bet he's never had a decent fuck out her in all his married life.

What to wear, I thought. Be daring, be bold and adventurous. It was a lovely warm day so I thought the white blouse and the black mini skirt. And that was it, that is all I wore. Oh for the sake of decency I had bra and pants, but I carried them in my bag to put on when I got to work. It excited me how I looked, the blouse was very thin and you could see my flesh through it, my dark nipples were particularly prominent and the excitement made them hard and erect. Standing in profile and catching the sun, which shone through the material you could clearly see the outline of my tits. This is going to cause sensation standing on the station platform I thought. The skirt just covered my modesty by just a few inches, *modesty,* that word again. Any bending, stairs or light breezes were going to reveal a sight to behold.

I parked in the station car park and pushed open the door. The two bays next to me were empty and a middle aged man was reversing into the third one. I swung my leg out and he caught an eyeful of my naked pussy. It somehow distracted him and his foot suddenly pressed the accelerator and he crashed into the car behind. Oh dear. Walking up to the ticket window I could feel my tits shaking about and I purposely exaggerated the effect. I could tell I was being watched and as I approached the normally sullen ticket clerk he managed to raise a smile. The effects of the admiration and my tits rubbing against the fabric of my blouse made my nipples harder and more visible. You could also see the areola around my nipples showing through. I was wanton and loving it.

Ticket in hand I skipped down the stairs to the platform. I could have used the escalator, but that would mean standing still, this way I could make my breasts bounce to great effect. Also there was a breeze coming up from the platform, and that, and my little skip made the front of my skirt lap up. I could see from the disembarking passengers coming up, that they got an eyeful of huge bouncing breasts and now moistening pussy.

I took my place on the train and off we went. It was a corridor train and I was in the compartment alone, unfortunately. A few minutes out of the station we began to slow down and looking ahead I could see there were repairs being done on the other track. Now's my chance I thought. I stood with my back to the window, spread my legs, bent down low and lifted the back of my skirt. The howls of delight were incredible as the workmen had the sight of my pussy as the train crept past. I undid my blouse and held it open shaking my huge tits at them. It caused great delight amongst them and as the train was now at walking pace they could all have a good long eyeful. One of them got his prick out and waved it at me. It was huge and just starting to harden. Oh I wish the train was slower so that I could see it at full blast. The train started to pick up speed again and I buttoned up my blouse and sat down. I fantasized about those workmen and thought of the next day, would they be expecting me to do it again? Could I even get off the train and spend the day with them, being fucked by each one of them in turn. All those huge dirty cocks inside me.

I sat quietly reading my book and fantasizing about sex. The door slid open and a man of about thirty came in. His eyes immediately homed in on my breasts.

'Morning,' he said, slightly self conscious.

'Morning,' I replied and lowering my book and sticking my chest out.

He was a well dressed guy, probably some sort of professional. I had seen him before on this journey, but not at such close quarters. Not a bad looking bloke I thought and wondered if he'd had his leg over this morning. As he sat there behind his paper I though, this is too good an opportunity to miss; I'm going to have fun with this guy.

I let my book fall on the floor in such a way that it rolled on his feet.

'Oh dear,' I feigned.

Being a gentleman he bent down to pick it up and as he rose I opened my legs so that he could not help but see my glory. I could tell by how he gulped when he passed my book that he had seen everything. He returned to his paper and I to my book. I let him stew for a few minutes while it sunk in as to what he had seen. He shuffled slightly in his seat and I could see he was discreetly trying to adjust himself. From the bulge in his trousers I could see he was getting a hard on. Within the next few minutes I will have that cock inside me I told myself. I then let my book fall again.

'Oh dear I'm so clumsy this morning.'

He immediately bent to retrieve it and paused hoping to get another look. I did not disappoint him, I slowly opened my legs before him and he gasped at the sight. I pulled my little skirt back so the sunlight shone on my moist lips. I moved my bottom to the edge of the seat and opened my legs wider. His mouth hung open in wonderment. I leaned forward and took his head giving him a long passionate kiss and before he got his breath back I guided his face between my legs.

'Lick me,' I ordered, and he went to it. I lay back on the seat feeling the ecstasy of his educated tongue teasing my clit. He was good. He lifted my legs onto his shoulders and clutching my buttocks he licked me like I had never been licked before. His tongue slavered between my lips and up, way up my cunt hole. He concentrated his attention again on my clit, licking it in a myriad different ways. Slow and fast, up and down and round about. Then he took my clit between his lips and sucked. It was too much, beautiful and too much. I could feel myself coming. I was coming slowly and I always knew the slow orgasms were the strongest. The feeling got stronger and I moaned with pleasure. He seemed to sense the stage I was at and timed his licking and sucking to tease this orgasm out of me. Eventually I came in full flood of pleasure crying out my joy. I clutched his head and thrust my hips, as if trying to push his whole body inside my quivering cunt.

As I heaved in pleasure he had swiftly dropped his pants and his teasing tongue was suddenly replaced by a huge throbbing cock. My legs were still over his shoulders so were now in the air as his huge prick slid inside my still eager cunt. I unbuttoned my blouse and his eyes bulged as he saw my gigantic shaking tits. As he thrust eagerly they shook even more which spurred him on to harder and faster thrusting. He gasped and I felt him expand inside me and I felt the force of his hot come inside my cunt. His prick squelched inside me as he filled me. I wanted it to go on forever, it was beautiful. I sucked his cock with my cunt extracting every last drop of come from him. It was brilliant. Red faced he got to his feet and clumsily made himself presentable. He took out his handkerchief and stood in dazed confusion unsure as to what to do. He was obviously a gentleman and offered it to me. I daintily but seductively wiped my dripping pussy. His mouth agape with fascination as he watched me. I handed it back and he wiped his cock with it. I had a vision of him sitting in his boring office sitting at his boring desk doing his boring job and secretly inhaling the sweet smells of sex from his handkerchief and reliving this wonderful experience.

111

But back to reality, I had achieved what I had set out to do. It was exciting doing it in a public place, the thrill of being found out. It was a corridor train after all I wonder if anyone passed and saw us. We reached our destination and we parted. I hope we meet again some day. Maybe he could bring a mate and we could have a threesome. Anyway we arrived at our destination, I went to the ladies room to clean up and put on my underwear, after all I have a responsible job to do.

BIRTHDAY PRESENT

It was about eleven o'clock when I arrived at Yvonne's, the door was ajar as she was expecting me and I walked in closing it behind me. Today was her eighteenth birthday, her parents had arranged a party for tonight but I wanted to get my tribute in first.

'It's me,' I shouted.

'In the bedroom,' came the reply.

I liked these morning meetings when her parents were at work and I couldn't wait to see her face when she saw what I had bought for her birthday.

I went into the bedroom and there she was on the bed absolutely naked.

'Happy birthday,' I said slowly gazing at this wonderful sight.

She smiled and just remained silent letting my eyes and mind drool over this wondrous sight. Yvonne was a buxom girl. Not fat by any means but she was well stacked with nice big firm tits and nice wide hips that you could really get to grips with when I fucked her from behind. She knew what I liked and she exhibited herself to the full, caressing her tits slowly with her hands, kneading them like bread and purring at the same time. She pushed them together and up. I loved to see her do that and she knew it. My cock was stirring as I thought of the times I had come over those great mounds of tit flesh. In my minds eye I could see my come squirting over them and running down the sides as she moaned with pleasure as she then rubbed my come over her tits like sun cream.

As she continued her tit massage she arched her back and lifted her knees and turned her hips towards me. Slowly and tantalisingly she opened her legs. Faster, I mentally begged her, but Yvonne liked the sexual power and used it to the full, and she made me wait for every pleasure. My cock was bursting for it. I took off my clothes and stood naked and eager in front of her. I saw her eying my throbbing cock. Slowly her legs opened and I could see her wet lips. I knew she wanted it because they were slightly open and I could see the glisten of her love juice. Her hands slowly slid down her belly and after what seemed an eternity, arrived at her pussy. Sliding her fingers between her legs she gently opened her lips wide. It was incredible I could she the juicy pinkness of her womanhood. I was aching just to dive between her legs and fuck her, but I thought no, I will tease her a little. But she hadn't finished teasing me yet and she slid her finger between her lips and slid it down to her tunnel of love and gently pushed it in accompanied by a gentle moan. Out it came and up between her lips to her clit. She gave a louder moan as her finger circled it then slid down between her lips again and this time she slid two fingers inside, then up to her clit again.

'Like it?' She said erotically.

My cock was aching for it and felt it would burst.

'I've bought you a present' and took it out for her. It was a twelve inch vibrator. It was incredibly lifelike with a huge bulbous end, a knobbly shaft that even had veins. I had already put the batteries in and it was ready to go. The clever thing about this one was that it had a little reservoir inside that you could put liquid in. In this case I had filled it with double cream. It also had a little heater inside, which at this moment was warming it, and the cream up to body temperature. And believe it or not, a come button at the base which would ejaculate the cream at the opportune moment. Very high tech and very expensive, but I thought it was worth it and looking at Yvonne's bulging eyes I think it was going to be money well spent.

She was still working her clitty with her right hand and her left hand was grasping for the vibrator like a child begging for a chocolate bar. I offered it to her and as she tried to grasp it, I snatched it back.

'Say please,' I said.

'Oh please, pretty please,' she begged.

I knew she was begging for it as she was rubbing her clit faster. I let her take it and it was as if an addict had been given a fix. She poised the huge knob end just touching her lips. They were slightly open and oozing love juice. She held the huge plastic cock with both hands. Gently she urged the knob end in and her lips gave way to surround it. As she pushed, it slid in and her lips opened wider. I could see it was a very tight fit, her lips surrounding it like a mouth. Inch by tantalizing inch it slid inside her and she moaned with pleasure even though it was stretching her to the limit. On and on it went further inside her. I was very excited watching and my cock was almost bursting with lust. Eventually it reached its limit and it started on its outward stroke. It glistened with love juice as her tight little cunt sucked at it. On and on she went slowly pushing it in and out and moaning with pleasure. She was using one hand now and with the other she continued to finger her clitoris. Faster and faster she went and I knew she was near. She looked at me with longing in her eyes.

'Jerk yourself off,' she said 'and come over my tits.'

I didn't need to be asked twice and I moved closer to the bed and obeyed her command. And as I watched her fucking herself with the vibrator I took my cock in my hand and give it the works

She was in a frenzy and she was crying out. I knew she was coming. She thrust the vibrator in and out faster and faster. She fingered her clit faster and faster. Her huge tits were shaking all over her chest then she let out an almighty shout of 'Oh God, I'm fucking coming,' which they must have heard next door. She pressed the come button and the warm cream shot like come into her cunt. Although it was an incredibly tight fit it squirted out of her cunt and dripped off the vibrator. It was fantastically realistic, so much so I could not hold myself back any longer and I felt myself coming. I shot my load all over her tits, it was incredible. I had never before shot so much come in one go, it covered both her tits. She moaned with satisfaction as she pulled the vibrator out. It was covered in cream and cream oozed out of her cunt.

Yvonne sat up and took my limp cock in her mouth and sucked off the rest of my come, which started making me erect again. Then she massaged my come into her tits. I could tell she wanted more so I got down on her and licked the rest of the cream out of her cunt. As she held her legs high and wide I licked and licked until she had another orgasm.

'Turn over for me.' I ordered.

She did so, kneeling on the edge of the bed and clutching a pillow in her arms. Standing between her bended knees at the edge of the bed I pushed her thighs further apart with my knees until she was stretched wide and I could see her gaping cunt still oozing cream. I positioned my rock hard cock just between her pouting lips and shoved it in right up to the hilt in one rapid thrust. Yvonne let out a cry of pleasure and I fucked her, I fucked her hard and she cried out as my cock pumped into her, my hands gripping her hips and pulling her hard onto my cock. Eventually passion overcame me and my cock spurted my second load of come into her. I held it inside her as far up as I could get. And as my erection died away my cream mingled with her cream.

Both exhausted we fell asleep arm in arm
'Happy birthday Yvonne. I love you.'

THE DENTIST

Today was the day I had been dreading. I had put it off twice, but now I had to bite the bullet and go ahead with it. I'm talking off course about the dental appointment. Now I freely admit that in many respects I am a poor excuse for a man, I even have the stomach gurgles when I go for a hair cut. This morning however I have got through a whole role of toilet paper and my backside feels like a peeled tomato.

'There's no need for this nonsense,' I kept telling myself. 'There's nothing to be afraid of,' I told myself unconvincingly.

Last year I got away with just a scale and polish but this year my luck ran out and I needed a filling, a whole filling. I quivered with fear. It was silly of course, I mean I had been coming here for fifteen or more years and had always seen Mr. Wilkinson, a most considerate and patient man. He had never caused me pain. Not physical pain anyway. It's just that feeling of things in my mouth that filled me with dread. That drill, that suction pipe, that mirror, all those fingers. Every time, within seconds of him starting, I was beginning to gag. A procedure that should take about five minutes took nearly half an hour because Mr. Wilkinson and his assistant could only work for bursts of five seconds at a time before that sinister croak would send them and their equipment reeling backwards in fear of a welter of last nights Vindaloo and chips.

It was unreasonable I know, as are all phobias. There must be something in my unconscious mind that was causing this and many times I had told myself that I would seek out some psychoanalysis and get it sorted out. But I always left it too late and the dreaded appointment was upon me.

I drove to the dentists as slowly as possible almost wishing I would encounter an accident on the way so I could cancel with a clear conscience. Alas it was not to be and in what appeared to be an unreasonably short time I was sitting in the waiting room with a magazine in front of me. I was looking at it but not reading it as my total thoughts were solely engaged in the trauma that was about to happen. What made me feel worse and more inadequate was that everyone else seemed cool and unfazed. A middle aged woman next to me cleared her throat politely and turned my magazine the right way up.

'Oh, th th thank you,' I stammered, and she smiled knowingly.

There appeared in the doorway a vision of loveliness with a short dark page boy hair style that framed her high cheek boned sculptured face to perfection. It gave her an almost classic French appearance. Her perfect hour glass figure was encased in a clingingly tight one piece uniform, with an almost indecently high hemline. A zip ran up from the waist and was left undone to reveal an ample cleavage that promised more.

'Mr. Peters,' she said in an incredibly sexy voice.

'Yes' I squeaked. My mouth dry with both fear and lust.

'This way please.'

She led me down the familiar dark and foreboding corridor to the chamber that I feared. I could almost hear in my mind the slow rhythmic beat on a snare drum, like someone being marched to the gallows. At the end, the open door of the surgery let out a beam of light into the dimly lit corridor. A grotesque shadow of the figure within was projected menacingly onto the corridor floor. The sound of a metal implement falling into a metal receptacle echoed around my brain. I was beginning to perspire.

'I'm afraid Mr. Wilkinson isn't in today.'

My blood ran cold at this announcement.

'Oh my God,' I yelped and stopped in my tracks.

'But don't worry, his replacement is very good. She's very experienced and we have had the surgery soundproofed.'

'Soundproofed.' No one would hear me scream I thought. I was now in a blind panic. And it was a *She;* I could see her evil shadow projected onto the floor again. A huge ugly thing six foot tall and as far across. Short cropped hair, a duelling scar and a jaw like Desperate Dan. Beads of sweat ran down my brow. I saw myself strapped to the chair suffering appalling torture, with everything bar the chair I was strapped to rammed into my mouth. I felt sick. I was about to turn and flee when the girl took my shaking hand.

'Don't be frightened,' she said in such a sweet sweet voice, as she took my hand and kissed it gently, 'I'll look after you.'

'Thank you,' I said weekly and feeling embarrassed. 'You're very kind er...?'

'Donna.'

'You're very kind Donna.'

'And the dentist is Julie, my twin sister.'

I was beginning to relax a little at this news and the vision of the orthodontic monster began to turn into something resembling a human. My relaxation was further aided by Donna, who still had hold of my hand and was kissing my palm then began to lick it which was very ticklish. She then took my middle finger into her mouth and she gave me a look with a naughty twinkle in her eye as she sucked my finger seductively. I was beginning to feel a stirring in my trousers as my pre med was interrupted.

'Save some for me.' Came the voice from the chamber.

And there in the doorway, in semi silhouette stood an exact replica of this alluring vision on my finger. Not only a twin but an identical twin. I quickly tried to stifle fantasies that were welling up in my imagination and tried to remember why I was here. I was half conscious of Donna releasing my finger and letting my hand brush past her breast as she released me.

'Do come in and make yourself comfy.'

Half in remembered fear and half in wonder I felt myself walking like a zombie into the surgery. There was the chair and I felt a chill run down my spine.

'Just sit down and relax Roger.'

Just that sentence made me more relaxed. That informality. Before it was always Mister this and Mister that. I sat there and couldn't not help thinking what beautiful women they were and they were identical, you could not tell them apart. And of course Julia had that same firm plunging cleavage. Her zip was also slightly lower than Donna's and I could see that she obviously had no bra on. Further casual examination led me to suspect that also that was the case with Donna.

'Open wide' ordered Julie with the syringe in her hand.

'Oh dear,' I gasped.

'No need to worry. I know you need something to take your mind of it.' She said.

And with that she unzipped her uniform and pulled it open letting her huge full breasts cascade out. And what a sight they were with nipples red and erect. I was so enthralled with them I hardly noticed her administer the anaesthetic.

'There, that will take a couple of minutes to take effect. So in the meantime enjoy the facilities.' She said leaning over me pushing her breasts forward.

I took them in my hands and fondled them, they were beautiful and all apprehensions of ten minutes ago had evaporated. I wanted this woman, I wanted her breasts. I sucked them and tried to get them into my mouth. But after a few minutes the anaesthetic took effect and my mouth was numb. Although my mouth was numb I could feel my cock was erect.

'Well I think you are ready now,' she said.

I could not believe what was happening, but it was certainly a change.

Donna was filling in my notes on the bench when Julie asked her for a new roll of cotton wool. She opened the door of a low level cupboard and looked for the cotton wool and I was treated to a spectacular view of her underwear. Actually they were very sheer frilly French knickers and with having a very loose gusset I had a good view of her pussy as she rummaged in the cupboard. It was a sight to behold and not what you would expect at the dentist's. As she extracted the cotton wool I could see the pinkness of her lips as they parted slightly.

The chair was lowered and Julie was about to begin. I told her about my fear of things in my mouth.

'Don't worry Donna will take your mind off it.'

I was about to ask why when she started drilling my tooth. Looking up I could see Julie's huge tits gently swaying before my eyes. As she continued to drill I could feel my cock throbbing and almost as if she knew, Donna was undoing my trousers. I lifted my thighs from the chair and she slid down my trousers and shorts to my thighs, my cock twanging to attention as she did so.

Julie's breasts continued to sway tantalisingly above me and as she continued working Donna came into my eye line and unzipped her front to reveal her equally huge tits, which she caressed and massaged before me in a very wanton manner. My cock was craving attention.

'There you are all finished. What do you think of the service Roger?' Said Julie.
'Wonderful.'
Donna started to work on my cock with her tits in such a manner I felt nearly ready to come over them. Then she went down on me and took the whole length of my shaft into her mouth and sucked me. It was unbelievable.
'No gagging this time Roger.'
She was right, no gagging. Well there was so much distraction.
'Look at Donna, she's got much more in her mouth than you had in yours and she isn't gagging.'
I looked down and Donna was sucking like a thing possessed. Her hair gently bobbing and her tits swaying as she went up and down my shaft. Julie presented her tits to me and I took them and sucked them. The pleasure was overwhelming and I could feel the flood of pleasure within me as I screamed out and let myself come in Donna's mouth. She took my load and sucked me dry.

'We will see you in six months time then,' said Donna.
'Mr Wilkinson will be back then' said Julie.
'Won't you be here?'
'Well he has offered me a partnership.'
'Take it and I'll be back next week.'

GREAT AUNT JUNE

It was a grey October morning as we stood by the graveside. The trees around us were in all their golden autumnal glory and a gentle rain began to fall. Great Aunt June was being laid to rest. She was the widow of my late Great Uncle Arthur, youngest brother of my maternal Grandmother. He was the success story of the family; a man who had made his fortune as a mining surveyor in South Africa and it was there that he had met and married June. His contract completed they returned to this country for a well earned rest before undertaking his next project.

Arthur was something of a racing driver of note and it was during one of his races when disaster struck. The tyre on the car in front blew and instinctively Arthur swerved to avoid collision, alas one of his front wheels hit debris causing his car to turn over and crash and he was killed. Now June was to join him in the great beyond and as I stood there I thought of the time twenty years earlier when I first met this remarkable woman.

I was seventeen years old and had not long left high school. It was the summer holidays and I was excited at the prospect of going to Sixth Form College. I must admit I had done pretty well academically but I was something of a shy loner so I didn't mix all that well with the other lads and not at all with the girls. I was quite tall for my age and although I was self conscious, it did have the advantage of preventing me from being bullied. Anyway that was behind me now.

Home life was quiet, Dad having died tragically young when I was about three years old so memory of him was vague, so it was just me and Mum. On this particular day Aunt June had phoned to tell Mum that she had been sorting through some things and come across some old photographs of Mum and Dad taken many years before and would she like them. So with Aunt Jane's address and a list of directions to get me there, I was despatched to retrieve the photographs.

I arrived at Aunt Jane's house and faint memories of Christmas's of years ago came into my mind. I pushed my bike through the gateway and up the long winding drive that formed an oval around the lawn up to the front door. It was indeed a very majestic home, not over large but majestic never the less. I knocked on the door.

Through the coloured glass of the door panels I could see the outline of Aunt Jane approaching. She opened the door and smiled warmly. She was, I was told sixty years old but she looked much younger. She had silver blond hair that was shorter than shoulder length and was cut so it curled around her jaw line. A long fringe just covered her eyebrows highlighting large blue eyes that sparkled and were wrinkle free. Although her immaculate complexion was pale, it had the texture I imagined that would in Africa change into a light honey tan. She wore a grey box pleat skirt and a close fitting floral blouse that showed of her curvaceous figure. A figure that was full and attractive. All in all a very pleasant sight indeed I thought.

'Hello Aunt June.' I said. 'I'm David.' I mentally bit my tongue at my unoriginal opening.

'My word you have grown into a fine young man. Come on in we've got lots to talk about.'

We went into the living room and I sat on the sofa. Aunt Jane came in with tea and cakes and we, or rather she chatted on about the family as people of that age are prone to do. Although a lot of what she said was of very little relevance or indeed interest to me I must admit I was quite fascinated by the personality and indeed beauty of this woman. She was sitting on my right and a small table in front of us contained the tea and cakes etc. The top couple of buttons of her blouse were undone and because of the way ladies garments tend to be buttoned I was treated to a glimpse of her ample cleavage every time she leaned forward. She noticed me looking and gave me a knowing smile as she caught my eye and I coughed with slight embarrassment.

'Do you have a girlfriend at the moment David?' She asked.

'No Aunt June not at the moment,' I answered somewhat taken aback.

'Oh call me June. This Aunt nonsense makes me sound older than I am.'

'You're not old, you are… you are, er, quite er, nice.' I felt myself cringing at my communication skills once again.

'That is very sweet of you David,' and she stroked my cheek with her hand, the skin of which was soft and warm. 'So you haven't a regular girl friend then?'

'Er, no.' I didn't like to say it but I have no girl friend full stop.

'Well there's plenty of time for that I expect when you get to college.'

'Yes.' I felt I needed to offer an explanation. 'You see I don't move in the circles where you meet girls. Being a loner, girls don't er.' I felt I wasn't helping my cause or my street cred so I changed the subject. 'Lovely tea.'

'Have some more,' she said leaning forward to pour and revealing her silky white plunging cleavage again. I gasped audibly and she gave that knowing smile again. She had the advantage over me and she knew it. She passed my tea and looked tenderly into my eyes.

'Have you ever been intimate with a girl David?' she asked in a seductive voice.

'Well, no,' I stammered. I felt vulnerable and at her mercy. Should I make an excuse and leave? I decided not to because although in some ways I'm ashamed to admit, I was slightly frightened, but on the other hand this woman attracted me greatly.

She sipped her tea and placed the cup on the small table. Turning towards me she placed her palms together and rested her hands on her lap and looked into my eyes again.

'Are you a virgin?'

'Yes' I replied slowly and feeling very embarrassed. But at the same time I felt relieved that I had admitted it.

With her finger under my chin, she lifted my head up.

'Would you like me to break you in?'

I thought for a few seconds about the magnitude of what she had said and I replied slowly as I looked into her eyes and said 'Yes June, I would,' and I emotionally melted.

Taking me by the hand she led me up to the bedroom.

The bedroom was large and luxurious and she sat me on the bed which was covered with a smooth silky duvet. She stood back a few paces and slowly unfastened her blouse and flicking it from her shoulders it slid down her arms and fell to the floor. Her bra was maroon in colour and it was very low cut and only just contained her very large breasts. Then she unzipped her skirt lowering it while still holding it and bending forward to step out of it. As she did so her breasts tautened and I could just see a tantalising glimpse of the coloured ring around her nipples just peeking out of her bra. I sat with mouth agape as she unclipped her bra and crossing her arms across her chest she took her bra straps and pulled them slowly from her shoulders to reveal the biggest breasts I had ever seen. I had imagined them to be big when she was fully dressed but now they were set free they seemed so much larger.

The experience was overwhelming. I could feel myself become erect. So erect it almost hurt and I had this strange pain in my back. There was more to come. Jane slowly slid her fingers into her knickers and seductively pushed them down, bending forward as she did so and let her breasts hang forward. As she let them fall to the floor and step out of them her breasts wobbled slightly from side to side. She stood up putting her hands on her chest and letting them follow the contours of her magnificent breasts and down to outline her wide hips. Her pubic hair was blond like her hair and I could clearly see the lips of her very desirable pussy. She was a magnificent specimen of womanhood and despite our forty three year age gap I felt I wanted this woman to be mine for the rest of my life. As she walked towards me her breasts gently swayed from side to side. Not only were they large they were very firm looking and stuck out majestically. Her nipples stood proud and must have been three quarters of an inch across surrounded by four inches of reddish brown areola.

She lifted me to my feet and commenced to undress me. When she pulled down my pants my erection twanged proudly to attention.

'My word what a big boy you have turned out to be,' she said sexily.

My cock ached for her. I stood at the foot of the bed as she slowly walked to the other side, gracefully sat down then lowered her head onto the silken pillow. Bending her knees she slowly opened her legs revealing her womanhood in all its glory. Her fingers slowly travelled down her stomach and reaching between her legs she pulled her lips open revealing the moist pinkness within.

'Let me rid you of your virginity David.'

I lowered myself onto her and she took my cock and guided it in, then grasped my buttocks and pulled the whole length of me inside her. The feeling was unbelievable and I had never experienced anything like it. My cock was inside a warm moist heaven and it almost felt it was being sucked. All my pleasure senses where on full blast, it was incredible. Each thrust was ecstasy, it was frighteningly beautiful. Too beautiful in fact because within a few thrusts I felt myself coming and with a scream of passion I came inside June.

I felt inadequate that I had not satisfied her. It was all too overwhelming.

'Oh June I'm so sorry to be such a disappointment.'

'Don't be silly, its human nature. The day is yet young and so are you. Just stay there.'

June went to the bathroom and I lay there feeling wretched. I had failed and my magnificent erection of a few minutes ago was limp and flaccid and a sticky mess. June returned with an old fashioned china bowl of warm water. Over her arm were draped towels and flannels. She put it all on the bedside cabinet. She soaked and squeezed out the flannel and rubbed it with soap. She then commenced to wash my sticky cock. The water was warm and soothing. After several minutes of washing she dried me with warm towels. This was the height of luxury I thought. What an experience. Not only that I could feel the desire coming back and life was certainly returning to my penis.

Putting her left leg on the bed and I could see my semen seeping out of her. June squeezed out the flannel and was about to wash herself. She rubbed the flannel around her pussy in a very erotic fashion. Then wringing it dry into a firm length she inserted it into her pussy pushing it in and out and moaning with pleasure. I was hard and ready for it again and June knew it. She threw the flannel in the bowl and got her leg across me. She was kneeling over me with her legs either side of my hips and lowered herself down. She guided my cock into herself and I felt it travel deep inside her.

'Fuck me June fuck me like you've never fucked before' I knew this was it and she rode me hard, I could feel her clitoris rubbing against my pelvic bone and she was in ecstasy. She had her hands on my chest and she fucked faster and faster her tits were now bouncing about with unrestrained abandon. On and on she went and at times I thought she would snap my manhood off, but she knew how far she could go and she took it to the limit.

I felt her cunt tightening around my cock and she screamed out in sheer pleasure. I had made her come and the thought of that was overwhelming and felt myself coming and we had our orgasm together.

I said I wanted this woman forever and I meant it. Despite the age gap we were lovers for the next twenty years until June's sudden but peaceful death. And as I stood by the graveside saying my farewell the rain mingled with my tears. 'Good bye my love and safe journey. I will see you again one day.'

A CHANCE MEETING

It was a beautiful Saturday morning in early autumn. The sun was cascading through the golden leaves of the trees and a gentle breeze made them whisper. I was indeed lucky living here, Warren cottage, left to my late husband and myself by his parents. Situated on the side of a valley overlooking a wide lazy river, it was situated just outside a small market town. Just far enough away to give peace and quiet but not too far as to make one feel isolated. A little way in front of the cottage was a long gone railway track that was now used as a bridle way. I thought back to the many happy hours John and I spent having evening walks along there with the sun setting over the river and the call of the wild fowl, Idyllic times indeed and it bought a tear to my eye to think that if he had lived we would have been our silver wedding anniversary next week. Oh well it was not to be. So the last five years it has just been me and Roger my faithful Springer spaniel.

As I stood drinking in the memories he gave one of those quiet little muffled barks as if to say get a move on. We strolled along, me listening to the birds singing and breathing deeply with eyes closed as I felt the cool fresh breeze on my face. Roger ferreted among the hedges and bushes doing what dogs do. Finally we reached the weir and Roger gave a sigh of disapproval as I turned to return home. We had almost arrived back when I noticed a man with camera around his neck climbing over a style a little way in front. H e strode over a small drainage ditch and came in our direction.
'Good morning,' he called.
'Morning,' I replied. And he passed by.

Roger seemed to take a liking to him and as he walked on he followed him, jumping up for attention. 'Come on Roger' I called. 'I'm so sorry, he doesn't usually…'
'It's quite alright. I had one just like him many years ago.'
I walked back to retrieve Roger as he had obviously formed an attachment, which is unusual as he is usually suspicious of strangers. Still if Roger likes him it must be OK. I have to admit the gentleman

was quite an attractive man, tall and mature, although a little younger than me, with a hint of grey around the temples. He put me in mind of a professional man.

'Are you down here on holiday?' I ventured.

'No I'm here for a conference, at the Black Swann.'

'Oh I see' I replied unoriginally. At least I was right about him being a professional. 'Very nice, the Black Swann,' I continued desperately trying to think of something to keep the conversation going because I somehow felt myself becoming attracted to this man.

'Yes it is, very nice.'

I felt the conversation beginning to dry up. 'Well.'

'Yes, well, I'll get along then,' he stammered.

I got the feeling that a bond was forming, but I felt frustrated that I could think of no way to capitalize on the situation. Fortunately fate was soon to take a helping hand.

As he turned to continue his walk he put one foot accidentally into the ditch, throwing him off balance completely and he fell to the ground with a yell. Roger was first on the scene administering comfort by licking the man's face.

'I say are you alright?' I said rushing forward to help him to his feet.

'I think I've sprained my ankle,' he gasped.

'Look, I only live just here, come inside and let me take a look at it. Here, take my stick.' And with that and a little support, we hobbled to the cottage, Roger wagging his tail approvingly.

I removed his boot and sock, bathed his foot in cool water to reduce swelling and bandaged it up. I spent many years as a nurse and I knew it wasn't a serious sprain, but I'm afraid to say I used my professional influence to ensure that I maximised the situation.

'It's very good of you to help me like this'

'Think nothing of it. It gave me a chance to practice on you. Oh, I'm sorry I didn't mean it to sound quite like that. I'm a retired nurse you see.'

'Oh right.'

'Er what line are you in?' I asked.

'Nothing as romantic as that I'm afraid. I'm in extruded tubing. That's what the conference is about, *new and dynamic advancements in heat set polymers.* '

'It sounds very impressive.'

'Actually it's as boring as watching paint dry. Unfortunately I drew the short straw to attend. Still it's over now.'

'So you'll be going home then?'

'Tomorrow. Its dinner and closing speeches by the sponsors tonight.'

'I see. Is your wife with you?' I ventured.

'Oh no, delegates only. Wife's would be more bored than we are, plus I don't think the sponsor's budget would run to that.'

I felt myself sigh.

'And anyway,' he continued, 'I'm a widower.'

My sigh took a u turn as I took in a deep breath of hope.

'To be honest with you I'm not looking forward to this evening at all.'

'Well it might be wise not to go, with your ankle being like it is. It might give out at any time,' I lied.

'Do you think so? It feels so much better now.'

'Oh yes, I do. Ankles can be very tricky you know,' I said lying again.

'Well I'd better get back and tell them the news.'

'No no. Phone from here, the less walking you do in the next twenty four hours the better. Complete rest.'

'Are you sure?'

'It's absolutely crucial,' I lied for the third time and Roger let out a mournful whimper as if he new I was taking advantage of this poor man.

'Just one thing' he said.

'Yes?'

'We haven't been introduced. I don't know your name.'

'Angela.'

'Derek. How do you do?'

'Fine thank you.' And we shook hands.

Thoughts raced through my mind; here I was with a strange man in my house. Thinking back over the events of this morning I could not believe what I had done. Formally I was resigned to spending the rest of my life alone with just the memory of John for company and against my better judgement I have picked up a man outside my door. Although I knew it was wrong, I also knew it was very right.

The evening progressed well and I cooked a meal for us and that plus the wine and port broke down any inhibitions. We sat on the settee with our glasses and continued to talk about this and that. Derek put his glass down and took mine and put it with his. He put his finger tips lightly on my cheek and I took them and kissed them. Roger gave a grumbling sigh and disappeared into the kitchen, flopping down with great dramatic *I am a hard done to martyr* attitude.

We looked deeply into each others eyes and Derek moved closer. His lips closed on mine and gently they met. We stared at each other again and he took my chin in his thumb and fore finger and gently opened my mouth. Our lips gently met again. His right arm slid around my shoulders and his left around my waist and he held me firmly and kissed me passionately. It seemed to go on forever and my mind was swimming with all kinds of dreams and fantasies. I would not have believed this morning that this would be happening now. I would not have believed I would have engineered the situation whereby I would have had the nerve to do this. I would not have believed that this would ever happen. But it is. I wanted it and it felt right.

Derek continued to kiss me passionately his heavy breathing making it take on a greater more urgent desire. His hands stroked my back and shoulders wildly as his lips massaged mine. I felt primitive desire rising up within me. An erotic tingle consumed my body. I wanted this man, I wanted his body. My body needed his. I felt his hand around my waist and his breathing became heavier as it crept up my side. I gasped in anticipation as it crept closer until I felt it cup around my breast and gently squeeze me. I put my hand on his and pushed it onto my breast more firmly and to show him that I wanted more, a lot more. As he fondled me it excited me immensely and I could feel myself tingling inside and I was becoming very moist.

I put my hand on his thigh and ever so slowly I let it slide ever higher. He continued to kiss me and I could hear from his moan that he was very excited. As my hand got ever higher I was soon to realise how excited he was. He shuffled slightly as my hand felt his scrotum, and a little higher and I could feel the full length of his erection. It was hard and throbbing and ready for action. I mentally promised it that it would not have to wait long.

I quickly unbuttoned his shirt and slipped it from his shoulders. He had a fine figure with a moderately hairy chest. I got up and brazenly unzipped his trousers and with one slick movement Derek lifted his hips and I removed his trousers and shorts in one go. His penis stood majestically and I couldn't take my eyes off it as I removed his one shoe and sock. He was naked except for his bandaged ankle. I stripped off slowly in front of him unbuttoning my blouse and throwing it aside. My nipples were hard and sticking out of my bra and Derek gasped at the sight. I must admit my figure wasn't bad for my age. I slid out of my skirt. I had on thick, thigh length black self support stockings and put my foot on the settee to take them off.

'No.' Ordered Derek. 'Leave them on.'

I obeyed. I reached round and unclipped my bra and very slowly and tantalisingly peeled it off. I could see Derek drooling and willing me to hurry up. I made sure his wait was worth it. My breasts were there for him and I purposely made them wobble from side to side for his titillation as I held my bra between finger and thumb and let it drop. I reached behind and undid my hair and as it unrolled I shook my head and at the same time I let my breasts shake again for his pleasure. Just my knickers stood between us and ecstasy and I slowly slid them down my thighs to the floor, bending forward so my dangling breasts showed themselves off. I stood up naked except for the black stockings that obviously had a particularly fetish fancy for Derek.

'Come to me.' He begged with arms out stretched.

I did not waste any time, I was aching to be fucked. I placed my knees either side of his thighs as he sat on the settee and pushed my breasts to his face. He took them both eagerly and sucked them with great relish trying to get them inside his mouth. It was beautiful as he sucked and nibbled at my nipples. I felt very excited and very wet and as he sucked at my breasts I urged him on.

'Suck my tits, suck them hard.' This rustic language seemed to instil greater lust. I let my fingers wander down to my clitoris and rubbed myself to ecstasy until I was almost on the verge.

'Are you ready for me Derek?'

'Oh yes. Fuck me. Fuck me hard.'

I lowered myself onto him, taking his shaft and guiding it into me, so his penis went in to its maximum penetration. I slid back and forth the action of his penis taking over from my self stimulation. It was unbelievable pleasurable and I could feel an orgasm building up inside me. The feeling took hold of me and it was overwhelming. The ripples of fantastic pleasure that took over my whole body were indescribable. At the same time Derek was also experiencing the same uncontrollable seizure of ultimate desire and we both groaned and gasped together in mutual orgasm. My pussy sucking Derek's shaft as he shot ripples of warm semen inside me. Eventually what seemed to last forever levelled out and we held each other in silence and wonderment.

Our relationship blossomed over the years and we are still together now. What little things like a chance meeting and sprained ankle can do to change the world.

Midnight Callers

It was midnight and I lay in bed unable to sleep. Caroline had dropped a bombshell tonight and told me it was all over, she had found someone new. She didn't mince words either, Carl was everything I was not, she said. Carl was heir to a chain of butcher's shops; he was rich and connected, drove a Ferrari and was athletic in every sense of the word. Not only that, but she would have free meat for the rest of her life. She also turned the knife in the wound by telling me about the eight inch piece of meat he had dangling between his legs. I felt at my lowest and it had come as a complete surprise, because I thought we were life partners and not so long ago talked about marriage.

'You're a nice man; you'll find someone else in no time,' she said patronisingly as she walked away. But she was right I was nice, that's my problem, nice and boring. I felt a tight lump in my throat and I'm ashamed to admit I could feel tears welling up. I had been cut, I had been cut deeply. I loved that woman and now she was gone. Should I phone and beg her to come back? I decided not, it would only lower me further in her estimation to see me beg. I turned over and tried to put it out of my mind. Tomorrow was another day, another opportunity.

As I lay there in that state halfway between waking and sleep, I was aware of a bright light outside that lit up the room briefly. A lightning flash I thought and lay there waiting for the distant rumble. It did not come but what I did hear was the sound of a window breaking and a loud hiss like a steam boiler being vented. I lay there quietly listening, it was silent. Then I heard footsteps, like shoes with metal tips walking across the paving stones. I dived out of bed and peered gingerly through a gap in the curtains. The patio and lawn were bathed in the blue light from a full moon shining between broken cloud. It was silent and still, with no sign of anyone. But I was sure I heard footsteps. And the breaking glass, what was that? I decided to investigate and crept down the stairs in my pyjamas and slippers.

I unlocked the back door and looked out. 'Hello, is there anyone there?' I whispered. I felt stupid. I mean if there was anyone there, would they answer? I picked up the torch and crept out. 'What was that?' I saw a figure moving in the shadow of the shed. I fumbled with the torch and felt a presence behind me. I was being compelled to turn and face this entity expecting to see a huge burly brute. Instead, my eyes fell upon the most beautiful woman I had ever seen. But before my mind could register her features I felt a sharp burning sensation in my upper left arm. She had something that resembled a mobile phone and it injected something into me. My mind began to swim and I passed out. I was aware of two pairs of arms lowering me gently to the ground.

My vision began to clear as I awoke. I felt confused, and then remembered the lurking figure and the beautiful woman who had burned my arm. Was it a dream bought on by my emotional trauma? I pushed away my pyjama sleeve and sure enough there was a pink patch of skin on my arm where this woman had injected me. I felt nervous, it all seemed very real, and I was in an apparently sealed room of off white metal. Lit by embedded bulk head lights and the walls were apparently seamless.

Standing up and trying to regain my sense of reality, I surveyed the scene. Nothing except the bed and bare walls. I heard an electronic hum and turned to see that same woman walking through the wall. I was stunned both by her beauty and her entry.

'I am Layla and we need you to help us Michael,' she stated.

What could I do to help her? And what help did she want? I quickly surveyed this perfect creature. She had short, almost red hair, with a fringe that was cut so that so that it was made of thin points of hair. Her pale skin and big eyes gave her the appearance of a beautiful Scottish lass. She was dressed in a one piece blue grey metallic suit that left nothing to the imagination. Large firm breasts with very erotic large erect nipples. The suit swathed her beautiful wide hips and moulded around the contours of her pubic mound highlighting her lips to perfection. To all intents and purposes she was virtually naked. I thought again about what she said, 'we need you to help us.' I could not help but think things sexual; but then considering my past record; it would take more than I've got to satisfy a woman like this.

'My help,' I stammered.

135

'Yes Michael.'

'You know my name.'

'We know a lot of you.'

I shivered. What could they want? I had visions of being taken over and released back into society as a merciless killer along with thousands more, so that these beautiful aliens could take over our world. 'What is it you want of me?' I said my voice beginning to croak.

'We require your sexual services, if you are willing.'

This loaded statement took some absorbing. No one has asked for my sexual services before, and, she said we, apparently meaning more than one. 'Certainly,' I said, trying to sound casual.

'Good. Then I shall make preparations.'

She touched the blank wall, and as she did so a red button momentarily appeared. I was puzzled as to why. Then as if to anticipate my question she started to explain the deal.

'We have come from a planet far away. A planet almost entirely populated by women. This is because of a genetic aberration that occurred thousands of years ago that caused a chromosome irregularity thus enabling only female births. Thereby making regular breeding expeditions necessary. We have scanned your biology and you have the perfect genetic factors that we need.'

I felt impressed and excited. 'Er how many of my services will you require?' I asked tentatively.

'On this expedition there are five of us,' she said matter of factly. 'We have little time and would like to start immediately.'

'Five,' I gasped.

'Fear not, we have something that will enable you to achieve our objective'

With that, another of these women entered looking almost identical to Layla only slightly thicker set and carrying another of those mobile phone things.

'This is Soo,' she said. 'She will administer the medication and be your first lover.'

The medication bit worried me slightly.

'Fear not,' said Soo. 'The medication will enable you.'

Enable me to what, I thought.

Without ceremony Layla took off my pyjamas and slippers and tossed them towards the wall and they disappeared through it. My wonderment was only curtailed by my acute embarrassment at my nudity. Now as I've indicated, my sexual prowess is somewhat diminished as is the size of my apparatus, this situation of which made it all the more diminished. Soo then put this unit to my arm and it hissed giving me a slight burning sensation.

'It will soon take effect,' said Soo.

'Over the centuries,' continued Layla, 'our bodies have adapted. We are able to become impregnated by a number of routes. Unlike your earth women who are fertilised through the vagina and cervix, we can absorb your semen through any part of our body including the skin. Plus also unlike earth women we reach fulfilment or orgasm as you call it not only through clitoral stimulation, but by the mere contact of your semen.'

I thought about this and thought, wow. But how long is it going to take to have sex with five women, given the time after sex it takes me to get steam up again. Layla once again pre-empted my question.

'The medication you have been given will enhance your sexual performance many fold. Not only emotionally but physically too.'

I wasn't really sure what that meant, but it sounded very interesting and also had many commercial possibilities I was certain.

'I shall leave you with Soo, and to your pleasure. I will return later.' And Layla departed through the wall as mysteriously as she had arrived.

'What is your pleasure Michael?' asked Soo in that voice I've only dreamed of.

'Whatever you fancy,' I replied somewhat unimaginatively.

With that she slowly passed her hands over her body, starting with her breasts. And as she did so her tight fitting metallic suit began to disappear. Her enormous breasts slowly began to emerge, then her nipples and as her hands passed over them they seemed to drop ever so slightly as if some invisible bra had just dissolved. She smiled at me as she let them sway slightly. They were large and firm and stood firmly with hardly any sag. She had lovely pale skin as Layla's and it seemed to highlight the reddish brown of the circle around her nipple which measured some four inches across. And her nipples were like ripe red cherries and just as succulent. As her hands travelled down her body her suit continued to dissolve revealing more beautiful pale cream flesh and her breasts still swayed tantalisingly gently for my pleasure.

Her hands travelled over her hips and she teased me as she went so slowly. She knew what I wanted and she made me wait. I could feel myself becoming erect and I could see she was eying me and smiling. A sudden fear ran through my mind, I hope I was up to the job I thought. My thought went back to Soo's slowly emerging pussy. And there it was in all its glory, the lovely white lips of her shaven pussy, or was it perhaps these women didn't have pubic hair. Anyway there it was, waiting for me. After that revelation her striptease soon finished and she was naked, and what a beautiful body she had.

She smiled at me; she had a beautiful face and a beautiful mouth. I took her to me and kissed her. She smiled again and sank to her knees. I looked down at this vision of loveliness kneeling before me. Then I noticed something that shook me. It was my cock, or my immediate thought was, it's not my cock. It was enormous. I took hold of it and normally I can hold it between my thumb and first finger. But I could barely get my fist around this monster. And its length. It must have been nine or ten inches long. What have they done to me I thought. Soo smiled once more and gently took my cock in her hands and kissed it. Then opened her mouth and took it in. It slid in and in. I'm going to choke her I thought. But I need not have worried as she gripped my buttocks and pulled me further in. This is not possible I thought but she took in the whole length without choking. What an incredible woman she was. She began to work me faster and faster my cock travelling its whole length into her mouth. I took her head and forced her harder and harder onto me. Eventually it was too much and I could feel myself coming and with a mighty thrust I pulled her head to me as I felt my come shoot into her throat. At the same time I felt her grip my buttocks and moan loudly as she also came. Slowly my still erect cock emerged from her mouth and she carefully sucked off all my semen devouring it eagerly as she did so.

She stood up and kissed me.
'Thank you Michael. I shall call my child after you,' she said.

I thought it an odd name for a girl, but in a world of women I don't suppose it mattered. She passed her hand up over her body and she was fully clothed again, smiled once more and walked through the wall.

This took some believing. I wasn't allowed to think for too long as another woman walked through the wall. This girl was just a lovely; the only difference was her hair was blond, but still cut in the same elfin like style. She was also taller and more slender, smaller breasts, but just as inviting, and wide hips and long legs that promised delights within.

'Greetings to you Michael, I am Val and I wish you well and hope that you enjoy me.'

I was warmed and fascinated by this affectionate reception. Val wasted no time and as she walked past me her hands caressed her body and her naked beauty was revealed as she passed. She lay on the bed and opened her beautiful long legs revealing her beautiful pouting pussy. Her knees were bent and her hands gently slid over her breasts and down across her tummy to her pussy. Gently she parted her already open lips revealing the beautiful moist pinkness of her inside. Her love juice was flowing and she wanted it. I wanted her too and was amazed that after just filling Soo's mouth I was still erect and ready for it. I don't know what they gave me but it was marvellous.

'You have a huge cock Michael.'

'Thank you.' I said, feeling somehow it was only borrowed. Borrowed or not, I was going to enjoy it.

'How do you say in your world Michael? Come on big boy and fuck me. Fill my cunt with your hot creamy come. I want it hot and heavy and my cunt lips are aching for your cock to suck inside.'

Her pillow talk was somewhat rustic but got the message across. I got on the bed and kneeled between her thighs. She moaned and writhed in anticipation, taking her breasts in her hands and fondling them. She looked gorgeous lying there consumed with pleasure even before I touched her.

'Fuck me Michael, fuck me. Stick your huge cock inside my cunt and fuck me and make me come.'

I didn't torture her any more and lifted her legs high and wide. She reached down and took my throbbing cock and guided it inside her. It felt tight but inviting and she screamed as I thrust the full ten inches inside her. She took it all and I felt her cunt sucking me. These women were truly amazing. It felt so good and marvellous and I looked down and could see my cock travelling its length inside her. She seemed to suck so hard it was almost impossible to pull out and when I thrust in it was like being drawn into a vacuum. It was so wonderful it was slightly scary. Eventually I could feel myself coming and as I pumped her faster and faster and harder and harder she yelled out with pleasure and shouted 'I'm coming, I'm coming. Fill my cunt with your hot come Michael.'

I did, and I felt it gush inside her. I heard it squelching I continued to thrust as my orgasm died down. I slowly withdrew my still erect cock from her relaxing cunt and as I did so I could see her cunt lips sucking my cock dry.

She sighed and rose from the bed. With a wave of her hand she was fully clothed again. She smiled and caressed my face with her hand. With a gentle kiss on my lips she disappeared through the wall.

I had just enough time to sigh when my next appointment walked through the wall. This time there were two of them.

'I am Tye and this is my sister Tay,' said the redhead.

'We are twins and we like to do things together,' continued Tay who was blond.

These two girls were really cute and the three in a bed situation was a long suppressed fantasy of mine which was obviously soon to be enacted. Both were probably less than five feet tall and Tye as I said was a redhead with a perfectly formed body. The only difference physically, apart from her blond hair, that set Tay apart was her absolutely gigantic breasts. I thought Soo's were large but they didn't compare to these. I was transfixed by them and I must have them. Without ceremony they both waved away their clothes and Tay's tits where around her waist. They didn't sag, they were just incredibly large. As they hung there they were wider than her body.

'You like them?' she asked.

'Very much so,' I drooled, my eyes sticking out as much as her tits.

'Then take them for your pleasure.'
I fell to my knees and buried my face in them, fondling and sucking and biting them. I cannot explain how it feels to be buried in so much tit flesh. It's obviously a man thing and I probably need therapy but I lost myself completely in her breasts. Both of them probably found it strange because I heard them both giggling.

I stood up and kissed her passionately. Because of her height and how her tits were hanging I could feel my cock between them. I looked down and there was my huge cock between these two mountains of tits that were peaked by nipples two inches across and areola that must have been six inches across the disc. I knew what I wanted and grasping each tit and squeezing them to my cock I tit fucked her. I stood there thrusting my cock between her huge globes. It was too wonderful for words and within minutes I could feel myself coming and for the first time I could see my come. It shot out like a volcano all over her tits and it continued to flow endlessly. It scared me I had never seen so much come. Tay screamed out in delight as I continued to gush over her tits. She was coming, the mere contact with my semen was making her climax. I continued to gush out all over both her tits and despite their huge size I completely covered both of them. It looked as though she had two pints of double cream poured over her tits. Not only was there such a lot, it came out with such gushing force.

She stood back slightly and she started to massage my semen into her tits, she doing one of them and Tye massaging the other. It seemed to be absorbed into her tits and as it was her head went back and she cried out in orgasm again.

Now totally clean she took her sisters hand and led her to the bed. Tye kneeled on the edge of the bed and bent down with her legs open. Tay kneeled at her side her huge tits draping over her sisters back and she pulled Tye's cunt lips open.
'Fuck her Michael. She's ready for you.'
I positioned my cock at Tye's cunt and eased my huge shaft into her cunt. She gasped in delight as inch by inch my cock slid inside her. Her

cunt was stretched tight as I went in deeper to its limit. And as I pulled back I could see her cunt sucking me. On and on I thrust and again before long I could feel myself coming. Tay sensed the climax and she gripped her sister's hips and as I thrust forward she pushed her hips onto me so I sank my cock deep into her cunt her tits shaking for my lust as she did so. We both came explosively with my come filling her cunt.

It was over, they dressed and left and Layla entered already naked. I lay on the bed holding my cock skyward. She stood over me and slowly lowered herself upon me. Layla was the most beautiful of all and as she took my length within her she smiled down at me. She kneeled astride me and lifting her hips up and down her cunt caressed my shaft. She did it slowly and with style. Looking down I could see her firm white lips gripping my cock. Then for the fifth time I shot my load deep inside her and we gripped hands in silent pleasure.

My job was done and it was time to return to my world and they to theirs. I was to be a father. I stood on the lawn and waved goodbye as Layla, Soo, Val, Tay and Tye went home.

I went back to bed. Tomorrow is another day, another opportunity. Layla had left me with a bottle of tablets containing the medication that they injected me with thus ensuring an interest in life.

THE ART CLASS

It was Tuesday night and Wendy and I were on our way to our art class. Tony and I had split up three weeks ago and it was her idea of taking my mind off men and Tony in particular. 'You need to broaden your mind Liz' she said. Her reasons were a bit suspect I think. Mainly because she just wanted someone to go to this stupid art class with her. As for her weak excuse about taking my mind off men, well that is an impossibility anyway and as for Tony well that was no problem because the twat is a wanker and this slag he's taken up with, well they deserve each other. She's the sort of tasteless whore that will that will suck him off then gargle on it. Good luck to them both.

It was pissing down with rain when we got to the centre and another exciting night of painting a vase of pansies lay ahead of us. Speaking of pansies I had hoped there would be some talent at this shindig but it was us two, a retired headmistress, Nancy the Goth, septic Sarah and gay Gordon. We settled ourselves at our easels for another riveting two hours of daubing. Monsoon entered in her usual fashion, clapping her hands together to get our attention and greeting us with her usual 'good evening girls and boys.' or in this case 'good evening girls,' would probably do. Monsoon wasn't her real name it was something unpronounceably East European. We called her Monsoon because as she talked she spit everywhere, which could cause havoc with the watercolours.

'No Sarah tonight Liz,' said Wendy. This came as a relief because she stank.

'Probably having an evening in, with a box of chocolates and her vibrator,' I replied with venom.

'Liz,' exclaimed Wendy, 'don't be awful.'

'Now this evening girls and boys, we will be doing something slightly different. I have been lucky enough to be offered the services of a life model.'

'Oh goody,' I said, thinking she has bought a cat along with her.

'Paul, would you mind coming through please,' she called out, and in walked this gorgeous guy with blond curly hair dressed in a towelling robe and rope sandals. Things were beginning to take a turn for the better.

'Just make yourself comfy on the chair dear boy.'

And without ceremony Paul slipped off his robe, kicked off his sandals and draped himself over a chair.

'Oh what a beauty,' murmured gay Gordon, obviously with designs.

'Now this is Paul everyone, who has kindly offered us his services for the evening to give you a different aspect to art.' Continued Monsoon, showering Paul with saliva. 'Now I'll give you all free range to interpret the subject as you see it and we'll see what pops up.'

'Oh I say,' whimpered Gordon, everyone knowing what he had that would pop up.

We made a start and all I could manage was a dot on my board. I couldn't take my eyes off Paul; he was gorgeous like a classical Greek God. Not an ounce of flab, just pure athletic muscle all over. Broad shoulders, nice biceps, a six pack, nice thick thighs and narrow hips. And all importantly a very generous cock indeed. As from time to time as he altered his position it was fascinating to watch it roll about slightly across his testicles. He even casually adjusted himself when he thought no one was looking, but I was always looking and it was a delight to see him draped it out so it lay comfortably across his scrotum. I kept fantasising about it. I mean it looked very ample now, how would it look when he had a hard on.

I decided to make a start on the picture and using charcoal I sketched the outline of his cock. I'll start with the most important just in case we run out of time. The proportions were all wrong of course and his dick filled the whole board. 'Can you just lower your left thigh a little Paul?' I asked, and this he did. I heard Gordon groan because now he couldn't see his cock properly. But I could and the manoeuvre worked and his cock rolled towards me. It looked marvellous and I could clearly see the outline of his bell end through his foreskin. I tried to imagine it when he was hard and ready for it, a magnificent ridge of purple throbbing magic. I could feel myself getting wet as I thought of that throbbing bell end on the end of that mighty cock thrusting inside my eager cunt.

I felt bold and I took a deep breath. 'Paul can I ask something of you?'

'Certainly, er...'

'Liz.'

'Certainly Liz anything.' And he said it in such an alluring way that urged me on.

'Would you mind pulling back your foreskin?'

Everyone gasped. But Paul without comment or embarrassment did exactly as was asked. He took his cock in his thumb and forefinger and slowly pulled back his foreskin revealing a mighty purple bell end that stood proudly. The shoulder of it was really wide and I could feel my face flush slightly at the sight of this magnificent cock.

'Liz,' said Wendy, partly amazed at my boldness and partly grateful for the view. Another added bonus was that now Paul's cock was significantly larger than it was a few minutes ago.

'Right, coffee break boys and girls,' said Monsoon looking at her watch.

Everyone got up to march down to the common room for a break.

'What can I get you dear?' said Monsoon to Paul.

'Oh nothing for me thanks. I've got a bottle of mineral water. I'll stop here and inspect the work so far.'

'OK, see you in fifteen.'

And Monsoon and the others prepared to troop out. Wendy got up.

'My turn for coffee,' she said

'Er, you go on. I want to finish this bit,' I said pretending to shade in. They all left leaving Paul and me alone.

'So how's it going said Paul coming round to see my rough sketch of a huge cock.

'Trying to get it true to life,' I replied.

'Oh, you flatter me a bit.' He chuckled at the huge cock.

'Not necessarily,' I replied looking lustfully into his eyes. His cock was dangling at my right elbow. I gently took it in my hand.

'Naughty girl,' he said gently.

'Well if the temptation is there, take it.'

I rubbed his cock back and forth and I could feel it hardening in my hand. He lifted my chin and kissed me then let his hand slide down my throat and down until I felt it slide into my bra and grasp my tit. He fondled me vigorously and gently tweaked my nipple which now was hard and ready as was his cock. He lifted me to my feet and kissed me with the urgency of someone desperate for a fuck.

'We've only got fifteen minutes,' I gasped.

'Better work quickly then.'

His hands slid up the back of my top and unclipped my bra. A second later bra and top flew across the room. Just as rapidly he unzipped my jeans and they and my knickers followed my other clothes. I was naked. He led me to a table. He kissed and fondled my nipples like a demon, then sat me on the table and gently pushed me back. Kneeling on the floor he draped my legs over his shoulders and kissed the inside of my thigh going slowly but surely higher. I mentally urged him on but he took his own sweet time. After eternity I felt him kiss my pussy and at the same time in my mind the sands of the hour glass were running out. Soon we would be discovered. This gave the experience an extra thrill.

His tongue lunged inside my cunt and I let out a little cry of desire. I reached down and opened my lips for him. Finding my clitoris he gave it all he had and very soon I could feel myself coming. It was marvellous, exciting, wonderful. The feeling gripped me and I was out of control. Ripples of unimaginable pleasure ran through my entire body. It built up to and incredible force and I let myself go with a single stifled cry. As the waves settled down I felt new heights as his huge cock slid into me. It went right inside me. I could feel it banging against the wall of my cunt. That gigantic, bulbous bell end rasping at the inside of my cunt stimulating me on, wanting more. He was thrusting harder and harder and faster and faster. The pain was pleasure. Eventually his bell end seemed to expand even further as he came and his hot come washed like a tidal wave of ecstasy inside my cunt.

Hands on the table and head hanging over me Paul and I were exhausted and satisfied beyond belief. I felt his cock slip out of me followed by a trail of his come. It squelched over the table as I sat up.

146

We quickly got our breath back, and got cleaned up and I got dressed. My face felt very hot and red and flustered when the others got back. Plus Paul's fading erection was still two inches longer than when they left. I wonder if they suspected anything.

I never finished my picture, but I did see Paul again many times. We're into photography now and maybe next time I'll tell you about one of our kinky films.

THE SHOPLIFTER

Today I was in a foul mood. Dave has dumped on me yet again and this time it's for the last time. I came home from work early, I had managed to get the afternoon off. A nice romantic afternoon I thought, a couple of pints in the pub with curry and chips and then back for a session of wild sex in bed.

Well I came in with the good tidings and Dave wasn't to be seen. I called out but no answer, bollocks I thought, he's gone out and here I am aching for a pint and a fuck. I went upstairs to get changed when I heard him grunting. Ah he's working out in the back bedroom on his multi-gym. I'll creep up I thought and pull his shorts off when he's holding his bars then get his sweaty cock out and torment him. As I crept up I realised he was in the front bedroom. I hope he isn't watching a porno film and jerking himself off; I want him to save it for me. I peeped through the gap in the door thinking I'll catch him doing it; them sneak in and finish him off.

He wasn't jerking off. Doreen from next door was with him. She was fifty two and that wasn't just her age, that was her bust size. She was kneeling on all fours on the end of the bed and Dave was stood behind her fucking her for all he was worth. Doreen was moaning with fake pleasure as her gigantic tits hung down and shook about. His shaft thrust in and out obviously on the verge of coming. He moaned louder and louder and thrust harder and harder making Doreen's tits shake even more. She was at arms length and her tits almost touched the bed. She was faking her orgasm to match Dave's because no body comes been fucked in that position unless you finger yourself at the same time. Dave soon gushed and he finished with his usual style. He pulled his prick out with his usual romantic style, his come dripping everywhere, then wiping it on the corner of the bed sheet. He went into the en-suite and I heard him peeing and farting. Dozy Doreen just rolled over onto her back and started fingering her cunt. I knew she faked that orgasm. Anyway she fingered herself off quickly and came almost silently as she screwed up her eyes in illicit pleasure. She sighed and just slumped on the bed. Poor girl, I knew how she felt; Dave failed to move me as well.

I was incensed by what I had witnessed; I wanted to burst in and confront them both and throw them both out naked into the street. But then I thought no I'll plan something more hurting. I crept back down stairs and decided to go out and I noticed Dave's wallet on the side board. I took out his credit card; I knew his pin number even though he thought I didn't. I shall have fun with that this afternoon and went to the supermarket. It was here that Doreen worked and I puzzled as to what to do to drop her in it. Shall I make a complaint about her at customer services? No that won't really do much to hurt her, and I would have to leave my name. No it must be something more subtle, but fiendish.

It was then that I saw Doreen's supervisor giving some juniors a tour and lecture of their magnificent supermarket of which she was probably telling them how lucky they were to work at such a notable establishment. What a load of shit, I wonder if she's telling them about the afternoons off when you can screw your neighbour's old man. I noticed from her name badge her name was Naomi. What a stupid name I thought. She looked the part I suppose, arrogant and thirtyish. Another one with big tits, it must be something in the water around here. She was fat though, I could see her calfs were thick and if the angle carried on up like that she must have thighs like tree trunks. She didn't dress to do herself any favours either. Her dark two piece suit was ill fitting, the skirt too long, mind you that might be to hide her legs. And the sleeves of her jacket were too long and her blouse too tight. Her tits were straining the buttons, and did she realise that she had a navy blue bra on under a white blouse. And the roll of fat cascading over her belt was almost comical. In short she was dressed like a sack of shit.

I spied my chance when she put her clipboard and mobile phone down on a pile of beans to explain something to her bored group. I reached over pretending to get a tin of beans and picked up her phone. I quickly moved to the next isle which was empty and hid the phone. I had the brilliant idea of reaching inside my knickers and shoved the phone up my cunt. It slid in nicely. I heard the commotion from Naomi and one of the girls said she saw me in the vicinity but could not be sure if I took it. I decided to take my leave. I went through the express checkout which was empty for once and fat Naomi was waiting by the entrance with a female security guard. Here we go I thought. It was the usual 'excuse me madam etc. may we examine your purchase.'

I was invited to the manager's office and told I was suspected of theft. Naturally I told them they were making a big mistake, but so confident was I that I gave them permission to search me. The master plan was beginning to take shape. I was taken to a little room by the security guard. She seemed slightly nervous; it must have been her first day. I intended to take advantage of that. 'Do you want me to strip?' I said in my best little voice.

'That won't be necessary madam,' she said politely.

But I was already unbuttoning my blouse and she coughed nervously. 'I mean you can't search me properly with my clothes on,' I said as I unclipped my bra and let it slide off. She began to look uncomfortable. I took her hands in mine and placed them on my tits and rubbed them up and down. My skirt was elasticised and with one swift movement, it and my knickers were on the floor. 'As you can see I have nothing,' I said seductively. Her hands were still on my tits and she had a glazed expression on her face as she drooled over my body. My hunch was right, she was gay. I pulled her head towards me and kissed her. I felt her tongue enter my mouth and I gently sucked her. She stated to breathe heavily and put her arm round me and fondled my tit roughly. I suddenly thought, if she goes for my cunt I'm done for so I went for hers. I lifted up her skirt and slid my hand down the front of her knickers. She parted her legs to let my fingers go between her legs. I found her cunt. It was warm, wet and eager and she whimpered as I gently teased her little clitoris.

I took her arms while still kissing her and sat her on the table. Pushing her back I lifted up her skirt and as she lifted her hips I pulled down her tights and knickers with one swift movement that took off her shoes as well. She was game for it and she gripped the back of her thighs, holding her legs wide open for me. I knelt down and gave her cunt the treatment it wanted. I licked her into a frenzy, giving it to her hot and heavy. I knew what I liked and I was giving it to her. On and on I licked her clit, driving her crazy with passion. There came a knock on the door, it was the manager obviously worried about the length of time we had been in here.

'Everything alright Sonia?' He called.

'I'm just coming Mr. Eversley,' she croaked. And with that she did come. She hissed and whimpered in suppressed orgasm. She wanted to shout out that she was coming but bottled it up. I kept licking her gently as she slowly came down.

'Oh God that was brilliant,' she sighed.

'Search complete?' I asked.

'Oh yes, search complete.'

We dressed quickly and returned to the manager's office.

'Nothing untoward to report Mr. Eversley,' she told him.

'Good. I'm very pleased. Naomi has obviously made a big mistake.'

'She certainly has,' I reiterated.

'Er will there be anything else,' said Sonia.

'No that will be all, thank you'

And Sonia winked and left the office.

'The silly woman has probably just put it down somewhere. I'll ring her number and see if anyone is in earshot.'

He dialled and I thought this could be awkward. It was, the phone started to vibrate inside me. He let it ring and the vibration was making me excited. This isn't a phone I thought; it's a fucking sex aid. The feeling was building, it was brilliant, here I was been given an orgasm by a man on the phone. It gave a whole new meaning to dirty phone calls. He went on completely unaware as to what he was doing to me. Keep going I mentally begged him. Keep going I'm nearly there. Just a few seconds more. And it started I could feel my cunt tighten around the phone, squeezing it like a hard cock. Sucking the come out of it. Up and up I went and I reached the top. I'm coming I'm coming I silently screamed to myself. Just a few seconds longer and I went over the top. I couldn't contain my silence and I let out a sigh of pleasure.

'Are you alright?' Asked a concerned Mr. Eversley.

'Oh yes just a touch of asthma. Bought on by the excitement I suppose,' I quickly answered. If only he knew he had telephonically just fucked me.

He put the phone down. 'Well I'm very sorry about all the trouble and embarrassment we've caused you. Of course in a situation such as this I will of course reimburse you. Would a thousand pounds be satisfactory?'

'Very satisfactory.' And I felt very pleased with myself.

Naomi entered. 'Ah Naomi you will be pleased to know this young lady has not got your phone and she deserves our most humble apologies.

'Oh I'm very sorry, madam,' She grovelled.

'I'm sure it will turn up.' I said.

'I even tried to call your number in case anyone heard it.'

'That wouldn't have worked anyway; I had it set to silent vibration mode.'

I smiled to myself as she said that.

'No if it had been on ring mode it would have played the national anthem very loudly.'

Well that saved us having to stand up I thought to myself.

I left with my check and Sonia gave me her phone number as I left. Just time to nip round to the car showroom and buy Dave a car with his credit card. I chose one that took his credit up to the limit. What a pity they didn't examine the card and saw MR. on it. Tut tut such laxity in security, obviously more concerned about the commission. 'It will be ready for collection within a week,' the nice man said. What a pity Dave has been disqualified.

I slipped back to the house and Dave and Doreen had got steam up again and were fucking. I put the phone in Doreen's bag. And slipped upstairs for one final look. Dave was lying on the bed and Doreen was sitting on top of him giving him her all. She was going at it so hard it looked like she might snap his prick off. It would serve him right. At least this time she looked like she was genuinely enjoying being fucked, if how her tits were banging up and down were anything to go by.

Anyway I left them to it and went back to mums for the weekend. The next day I phoned security at the supermarket to tip them off about the stolen phone in Doreen's bag. This led to a further security investigation and it transpired that Doreen had a scam going and was sacked prior to prosecution. Plus it's nearly the end of the month so Dave will soon get his surprise car and credit card bill. Nice how some things turn out isn't it?

SHOPPING DELIVERY

I pulled into the drive and was glad it was Friday. Tom would be home about three this afternoon and we were off for a weekend break in the Lake District. A romantic dinner in Mario's tonight and a whole days walking ahead of us tomorrow. As I stopped I heard one of the carrier bags slide over in the boot. I noticed Julie's car in the drive next door. Good, I thought, I'll nip round with her stuff and have a leisurely hour catching up on the local gossip.

I got out and opened the front door and ferried everything through to the kitchen and deposited everything onto the table. It wasn't my usual big shop as we didn't need anything for the weekend food wise. It was mostly tinned and frozen stuff and a few things to tide us over during the week. Shopping away I nipped round to Julie's with her stuff.

I walked around the back and in through the always open back door and announced myself. No sign of her. I walked through to the lounge to the stairs and shouted up. The shower was going so I returned to the kitchen and started putting her shopping into the fridge and put the kettle on. I heard the bathroom door close and activity upstairs. The kettle was beginning to warm up and I was just putting the last few items away as Julie entered the kitchen behind me. 'I've put the kettle on and put your Barbeque things on the bottom shelf. There was a two for one offer on the...'

As I turned I got the shock of my life. Before me was a naked man. All sorts of thoughts ran through my now panicking mind. Had he murdered Julie and a similar fate was to befall me. Or was it going to be a fate worse than death. I just gasped and was unable to speak. I saw the bread knife on the table and my thought was to grab it and get in the first blow before it was too late. Those few seconds passed like hours with imagined scenarios that were too dire to contemplate.

'Who are you?' He asked in the trembling voice of what a murderer, I had imagined would sound like, after the dastardly deed had been discovered.

154

'I'm Helen from next door,' I replied, my eyes wide open in terror and my hand edging closer towards the kitchen knife.

'I didn't realise anyone was here.'

'Obviously,' I replied, one eye on the knife and I'm afraid the other eye on this naked body. And I'm also ashamed to admit that the other eye was rapidly losing interest in the knife for the other more heady delights that the other one was enjoying.

'I'm Robert,' he blurted.

And the feeling of ultimate terror was now fading away to be replaced by one of acute embarrassment.

Robert was Julie's son. He had been living in America for some years, and as Julie and Steve had only been living here for three years, I had never had the opportunity to meet him. Although Julie had talked about him endlessly, saying how well he was doing, plus all the photos, you never really spot the resemblance when they are naked with shower tousled hair. A silence fell, and in those few seconds before Robert realised that he was still naked and grabbed a towel to cover his modesty, my mind scanned in for posterity the image of this incredible body a generation earlier than mine.

'Oh God, I'm so sorry,' he said securing the towel. 'I didn't hear you come in.'

'I did shout upstairs. I heard the shower and assumed you were Julie.'

His hands were trembling and his fumbling with the towel proved ineffective and it fell to the floor. So I was then treated to another few seconds glimpse of this magnificent young mans body. He had thick dark curly hair, a firm square jaw, dark eyes and an all over gentle tan giving him a Mediterranean appearance which I found very compelling. His shoulders were broad and muscular but not as a body builder but as an athlete. His stomach was flat and firm, with what I believe is called in the modern parlance 'a six pack.' He had thighs like a footballer, the muscles which rippled as he struggled with his towel, leaving one of his thighs seductively revealed by the slit in the towel. Finally his calf's bulged and tapered down to a narrow ankle. As for the bit between six pack and thighs. Well it was almost too magnificent for words. His scrotum was the size of a tennis ball and his penis dangled, gently swaying about as he continued to struggle with his towel. It must have been a good five inches long and very majestic. I was ashamed of myself as I tried to imagine its size when fully erect. And was even more ashamed of myself when I tried to imagine what it would feel like inside me. The tip of his penis peered out cheekily from his foreskin, which against the sunlight coming through the window highlighted the broad rim of his ample and bulbous glans through the skin. It fascinated me enormously as I mentally visualised myself pulling back his foreskin to reveal his wonderful purple end.

Tom was circumcised so his glans was on show all the time, so it didn't have the unwrapping value as it were. I realise of course, when erect the foreskin peels back of its own accord, but it was always fascinating to catch a penis at its early stage of arousal and unwrap your present. I coughed with embarrassment as I tried to suppress these wicked thoughts. I was after all a happily married woman of twenty seven years and been absolutely true to the day, and this magnificent Adonis was the son of my best friend and a whole generation in age difference.

'I'll go and get dressed,' he stammered. 'I only came down to put the kettle on.'

With that he turned and headed back upstairs and as he did the towel came off again and I was treated to the sight of two tight muscular buttocks.

'I'll see to it,' I shouted after him. 'Tea or coffee?'

'Tea please,' came the distant reply.

The kettle had now boiled and I made the tea. My mind was still swimming with the emotions and sights of the last few minutes and I felt a tingle of excitement within me. A feeling that I had felt before many years ago when I felt my fidelity was being tested. If I was not careful the events of this afternoon may test it once again. I made the tea.

Within a few minutes Robert returned wearing a towelling bathrobe and clutching his hand which was wrapped in a handkerchief.

'Oh Helen I've cut my finger,' he whimpered, like a helpless child.

'How did you manage that?'

'I knocked over the toothbrush glass and I cut myself picking it up.'

I opened the tall cupboard in the kitchen where I knew Julie kept her aspirins and other medicines and found a box of plasters. I quickly inspected the wound and selected an appropriate plaster. I took his wounded hand in mine and held it close to me as I stuck on the plaster and carefully wound it round his finger. I continued to hold his hand with both of mine as I smoothed down the edge of the plaster. 'That should do it,' I said still holding his hand.

'Thank you,' he said with emotion.

I looked into his face and then back to his hand. He had that look, that look that I recognised, that dangerous look.

'It should be alright now,' I whispered, and looked into his face again.

He didn't speak; we just looked at each other. I was still unconsciously holding his hand, little realising that I was virtually clutching it to my bosom. I don't know why I did it but I held it to my breast and I felt his fingers move around it and gently cup it. Oh god what am I getting myself into I thought. With his other hand he lifted up my chin and our lips met. I found myself just dissolving into the situation. We kissed long and passionately and I knew where destiny was taking me. I knew it was wrong but I knew I was going. Robert stood back and took my hands in his.

'Come to bed,' he said gently.

And I let him lead me upstairs.

He stood by the bed and unwrapped his robe and let it fall. He was naked again, but this time without the embarrassed fumbling. This time it was with purpose and with confidence. My fingers trembling I unfastened my blouse. Robert stepped forward, gently took hold of my blouse and ripped it open. It shocked me and thrilled me at the same time. He deftly undid my skirt and I felt it disappear. He took me in his arms and kissed me and I felt his now very erect penis pressing into my tummy. As he kissed me I felt him unclip my bra and I lowered my arms to let it fall away releasing my breasts for his pleasure. He took them in his hands and fondled them as he continued to kiss me passionately. I was eager and I wanted to feel his body within mine, I wanted to be taken with fiery passion. I felt the love juice flowing within me, welling up and eager for satisfaction. I stood back from him and slowly slid down my knickers, at the same time leaning forward so my breasts would hang down for his admiration. Although approaching fifty my body was still in reasonable condition. And as I kicked away the final frontier and stood as naked as he, I heard a gasp of approval. His bulbous glans was now well clear of his foreskin and this mighty object of desire was throbbing with pent up lust. A lust that I would satisfy.

I decided to take the initiative. I lay on the bed as he stood at the foot watching me. It thrilled me to know that he was enjoying me and I could see his cock throbbing with every pulse of his heart. I wanted that cock inside me, deeply inside me, but I wanted more teasing first. I bent my knees and slowly opened my legs for him. Again he gave a gasp of delight. With a gentle and seductive moan I let my hands flow over my breasts, pushing them up to give maximum cleavage. Massaging them for his delectation. Then I let them slowly slide down my belly and my fingers slid between my legs to my pussy and gently and teasingly I held open my lips which were now very moist and ready for attention.

Robert seemed really turned on by my performance and in turn rubbed the length of his shaft slowly with his right hand. I let my middle finger travel down the length of my lips to my vagina and gently let it slide within the moist warm tunnel of love. I then let it go on a return journey until it found my clitoris and I gently fingered myself. Robert was shuffling about in sexual desperation. I held the backs of my knees so my legs were open to their maximum.

'Lick me.' I commanded. 'Lick me until I come.'

He didn't hesitate. He virtually dived on me and buried his face in my crutch. I felt his tongue explore me. Deeply thrusting in and out. It was wonderful and I howled in ecstasy. He then turned his attention to my clitoris and licked it voraciously. It was unbelievably erotic and I knew I couldn't take much more of this until the inevitable happened. But Robert knew his stuff, he knew what a woman wanted and he licked me to the edge. Orgasm was just a few tongue strokes away. I was on the brink and he knew it. I needed just a few hard licks to send me over the top.

'Harder please Robert, harder.' I begged. But he left me suspended. 'Please Robert please.' I begged once more. And with two more hard licks I went over the top and that cascade of uncontrollable pleasure gripped my whole body and I descended into an explosive orgasm and I screamed out my pleasure. He continued to lick me earnestly and the orgasm went on for an almost frighteningly long time. I was gripped with pleasure and was helpless. He continued tonguing me as a welter of pleasure went on and on. Eventually it began to subside and I began to come back to earth. This was the signal for the second phase and wiping his mouth Robert kneeled between my legs and mounted me. He took control of my legs lifting them up to his shoulders and positioned himself to fuck me. I reached down for his cock and guided it into my still eager cunt. He did the rest and his huge cock slid inside me. A magnificent feeling and although I had come already I still wanted it. He thrust in and out like a demented demon and I could feel my tits shaking about in abandon.

'Oh Helen you feel wonderful, too wonderful. I can't hold it much longer.'

And with a few more thrusts that felt dynamic and went deeply inside me, I felt his cock dilating as he shot his hot come deep inside my eager cunt.

He collapsed in near exhaustion at my side. Rightly or wrongly I had done it. It was an experience and I don't feel any the less for Tom. He was my husband and I love him deeply but I needed the experience that Robert gave me. It never happened again and I've spoken to no one about it. It's all part of life's rich experience.

FAITH IN THE FUTURE

We had just dropped the girls off at school and were on our way to the supermarket for our weekly shop. I felt very lucky in many ways; we had two lovely daughters, Kate thirteen and Linda fifteen. I was married to Leo the most wonderful and considerate man in the world. Nothing was too much trouble for him and he would do things that other, lesser men would baulk at. I awake every morning and thank God for giving him to me. I have a lot to be grateful for and I have everything that is precious except for one thing. My sight. I was hit by a car when I was eight and have been blind ever since. So I depend on Leo a great deal. The sad thing is, I've never seen what he looks like, true I can feel the contours of his face and his body and the same with our lovely daughters, but I pray that one day that I shall be able to see them. From when they were born Leo has photographed and filmed their total lives and it keeps me going when he promises that one day we will sit in front of the fire and go through this photographic life. I pray for that day to come.

There is hope; in fact I was fortunate enough to have been referred to a specialist who has developed a pioneering technique in treating my kind of blindness. I hope you will forgive the loose medical terminology but I don't really understand the technicalities other than there is a possibility that my sight or most of it could be restored. I underwent some tests three weeks ago and since then I have waited with baited breath for the results.
'Here we are Faith,' said Leo.
'What,' I replied somewhat distant.
'The supermarket.'
'Oh sorry, miles away.'
'Don't worry things will workout.'
Leo must have read my mind. 'Yes, let's hope so.'
'Faith by name, Faith by nature,' he reassured me.

Well we did the shopping followed by the usual tea and toast in their cafeteria. It's a strange ambience sitting there listening to the sounds and smelling the smells. The bacon, the sausages, the fried eggs. Smells that

I can put pictures to. I don't suppose those things have changed in thirty years. But what about the check out tills, computers, mobile phones. All making strange sounds, what do they look like?

'Penny for them.'

'Sorry Leo, I'm not much company today.'

'Never mind, drink up and we'll get of home.'

I felt the front door push a pile of mail as I opened it. Leo followed me through and picked it up.

'Anything?'

'No just bills and junk I'm afraid. Don't worry it will come.'

I heard the mail land on the settee and Leo took me in his arms. I felt tears welling up in my eyes.

'Oh what if...'

'It will be OK I know it.'

Leo was a tower of strength and he was wonderful. He hugged me closer and I sniffed away the tears. He took out his hanky and dabbed my eyes. Then he kissed me. One of those long loving meaningful kisses. I put my arms around his shoulders. He started to kiss me harder and I could feel the passion welling up in his body. His hand which was around my waist started to slide up my side. I knew where it was going and what Leo wanted. It made my whole body glow. I could feel my breasts tighten and my nipples become erect. And also that tingly moist feeling inside my vagina. I let my left hand slide down Leo's body until I found his buttocks. At the same time his hand found my breast, kneading it passionately, breathing ever deeper, as he continued to kiss me. He found my nipple sticking through my blouse and rubbed it with his thumb and forefinger making it glow and become more erect.

'Let's go to bed,' he murmured. He took my hand and I obediently followed.

He started to undress me, my unbuttoned blouse falling to the floor. He unclipped my bra and gently taking my straps let the garment fall away. It felt good to have them exposed and I could tell by his gasps that they gave him pleasure. I shook them gently so they would swing seductively for him. I unzipped my skirt and let it fall, followed by slowly sliding down my panties. I stood before him. 'I'm yours Leo.'

I heard him rapidly remove his clothes, then his warm body embrace mine. I could feel his erect penis against my belly. He kissed me and fondled both breasts at the same time. I felt his arm slide around my back and his other slide behind my thighs and he swept me of my feet and carried me to the bed and laid me there. Lying next to me he took each breast in turn and sucked them. He continued to suck and kiss them as his hand slid slowly down my tummy.

'Open your legs for me Faith,' he murmured.

I did so and I felt his exploring fingers run between my lips. His middle finger found my vagina and he gently let it slide in and found my g-spot. It was joined by another finger and then a third; it was a tight fit that hurt a little. He then moved his fingers about, shaking me from the inside. I felt his fingers slide out of me and then pass between my lips until it found my clitoris. And very gently and delicately he worked on it, rubbing me up and down and round and round. Teasing me wonderfully. It was becoming too nice, so I gently brushed his hand away and found his penis. I let my hand gently stroke the length of it. It felt big and hard and his bulbous end particularly fascinated me. I liked to feel the extended ridge that went around the top. I imagined this broad ridge stimulating the inside of my vagina. Rubbing and stimulating the sides with every thrust, this ridge of pleasure, this collar of lust exciting my womanhood to ecstasy. This ridge touching my clitoris with every lustful stroke, each one building me up to an inevitable climax. I felt the tip of his penis and it was moist with semen aching to be released. I lowered my mouth to meet his shaft. I felt his drop of semen on my lips. I opened my mouth and took it in. My lips encircling this magical bulbous end, feeling the wide ridge pass between my lips and as I sucked my lips flowed over it. Leo moaned with pleasure. We were ready.

I got up and sat astride his hips and guided his mighty penis into my vagina. I slowly lowered myself onto him, taking his shaft slowly inside my body until I could feel his full length inside me. Then raising myself up until I could feel he was almost out then lowered myself down again. Leo moaned with pleasure and I speeded up my thrusts which tantalised him even more. It was exciting and extremely erotic. I could feel my breasts bouncing about uncontrollably. As I thrust up and down on Leo's rock hard penis I let my finger find my clitoris and I self stimulated myself. That combined with my thrusting was overwhelmingly pleasurable and I felt orgasm approaching. It welled up inside me and I screamed out with the intoxicating all consuming pleasure of it. Leo climaxed seconds later and I felt the powerful thrust of his semen gush inside me. The passion gently subsided and Leo slowly slid from me. We lay there arm in arm, in love, together.

A little later as we lay there the phone rang and Leo reached for it.
'Hello... yes... one moment. It's for you.'
'Hello.'
'Mrs. Jackson?'
'Yes.'
'It's Dr. Barnes. The best possible news. Your test results show that surgery would in all probability be most successful.'
'You mean I'll be able to see again?'
'There is a ninety five percent certainty that you will be able to see your Christmas dinner this year.'
'That's wonderful news, I'm so pleased.'
'Good. I thought I would let you know as soon as possible, so if you can come and see me we will make arrangements.'
'Yes I will and thank you so much.'
'My pleasure. Good bye.'
'Good bye and thank you once again.'
'Good news I take it,' said Leo, with some understatement.
'The best. He says I'll be able to see by Christmas.'
'That's wonderful. I'd better get my hair cut then.'

It was indeed wonderful news; I would see Leo and the girls. And I would be able to see that penis that has given me such pleasure over the years.

BANK BALANCE

Another day, another mundane day, I thought as I stepped dripping out of the shower and stood in front of the mirror and sighed. What a sight, I was forty eight, which was both my age and coincidently my bust size. The latter of which may sound appealing but unfortunately I had a stomach and hips that almost matched it. I held my stomach in and stuck my chest out and it looked acceptable, even something resembling appealing. But to be realistic, I couldn't hold my breath for the rest of my life. I gave a sigh as my held breath blurted out and my stomach came out and my huge tits sagged down to rest on the top of it.

I towelled myself dry as I once more reviewed my life. I was the wrong side of forty and divorced, a marriage that ended after eighteen years when John decided he needed a newer and faster model. It wasn't an exciting marriage I admit, but it was steady, for John too steady. His excuse was that he wanted more excitement to our sex life, well so did I. I just went along with his wishes, which was the same routine. It usually started with a surprise grope of my tits, and then a rough hand thrust up my crutch, a kiss if I was very lucky. Then he was on me and up me in the missionary position, always the missionary position. A few thrusts and grunts and a sigh from him then he rolled over, satisfied and went to sleep. Occasionally if he was feeling romantic, he would ask how it was for me and normally he was snoring before I could give the answer. In truth the answer was, it was not alright for me, it was frustrating and I was left lying unsatisfied in a sticky mess.

He had the audacity to blame me for a boring sex life. Anyway life goes on and fortunately I have my career in the bank. Only a small regional bank not one of the majors, but at least I was the manager, so that was something. However from a social point of view life was not so interesting, because of my age and shape I was not often invited out by young men. To be honest I was not invited out by middle aged men, or even old men. In fact the only social gatherings I attended were connected with the bank and always going alone I felt somewhat uncomfortable and usually left at the earliest respectable opportunity.

I rubbed myself over with talc, the aroma made me think of my childhood. Ah, happy innocent days. As I caressed the talc into my breasts they flowed over my hands like large balloons and I longed for some hero to do this for me. I rubbed them both, lifting them up and pushing them together and manipulating them. My nipples started to harden as I did so. 'Not bad tits.' I thought as I shook them and watched them sway then assume their resting position. I shook a handful of talc onto my palm and gently massaged it between my legs. It felt smooth and sensual as the talc coated my labia and as my fingers slid over my lips and my clitoris it gave me a little tingle. It longed for attention and I wondered if ever again it would receive a man. I toyed with the idea of lying on the bed and reliving a fantasy but then again I had just had a shower and I had an exciting day ahead of me at the bank.

It was gone five thirty and business at the bank was over. Customers and most of the staff had left, it was just David Roberts my chief cashier, putting the last of the cash and cheques in the vault in the main hall, and me finishing off letters for tonight's post, in my office. It was at this time of day after the bank had closed and before the cleaners arrived at six that I had time to think and reflect. However this afternoon fate was to take a hand. I was signing the last few letters and thinking I could get away early when I felt the jolt of my bra strap snapping. 'Damn' I thought. Then was thankful it didn't happen earlier. It would have been very embarrassing showing the party from head office around with one tit three inches lower than the other. I decided to take it off then if I kept my jacket on and buttoned up no one would notice and the jacket would stop them wobbling about when I walked to the car.

I quickly unbuttoned my blouse and took it off. My left tit was almost hanging out of the cup. I unclipped my bra and dropped it on my desk. I caught my reflection in a mirror I have on my dressing cupboard and like this morning I was admiring my tits, caressing them and pushing them up and out and my nipples began to harden again. I stood in foolish admiration when the door suddenly opened. I let my tits drop and I felt them uncontrollably swinging about as I snatched my blouse to quickly cover myself up.

'Oh, I do beg your pardon Mrs Chaplin. I shall return when it's more convenient.'

It was Mr. Roberts my second in command, a very proper gentleman of the old school. The exact image of a bank employee that used to be characterised in old movies. I felt very embarrassed and it was my own stupid fault for prancing about like a sixteen year old. I felt hot and my face was flushed as I quickly made myself decent.

A few minutes later there was a knock on the door. 'Come in,' I croaked clearing my throat.

'I cannot apologise enough for entering unannounced earlier,' said Mr. Roberts.

'It quite alright. I just had a mishap with my underwear,' I burbled somewhat embarrassed. 'I'm sorry you had to witness such a hideous sight.'

'Not at all Mrs. Chaplin. You do yourself a grave injustice. If I may be so bold you posses a most beautiful pair of breasts.'

'Er, thank you,' I said somewhat surprised and flattered by his compliment. I had always considered him someone with a stiff upper lip and now I was thinking he might have a stiff something else.

I was ashamed at the thoughts running through my mind. I looked at my watch; the cleaners would be here in twenty minutes. Mr. Roberts looked at my damaged bra on the desk and I quickly bundled it into a drawer. 'Sorry,' I said again.

'Not at all,' he said with a knowing smile. 'Everything is secure and here are the keys'

I stood up to take them from him and he placed the keys in the palm of my hand and gently closed my fingers around them. He continued to hold my hand and our eyes met. I let my hand slip out of his and I began to feel that tingle again. 'I'll put it on my ring.' And I unbuttoned my jacket without thinking to secure the key to my skirt belt. As I opened my jacket and swung it back I heard Mr. Roberts gasp quietly. He could see my tits through my almost transparent white blouse. 'Sorry,' I said again for the countless time that afternoon.

'No need to apologise Mrs. Chaplin.'

'Judith, please call me Judith.' I said, my voice quaking somewhat as I pulled my jacket together.

He sensed the mood and walked towards me and took my chin with his hand. My heart began to thump and I felt my legs turn to jelly as he kissed me passionately.

'The cleaners will be here in fifteen minutes,' my voice now wavering with desire.

'Then we must proceed swiftly.'

He slid my jacket from my shoulders and took me in his arms and kissed me with a greater passion. I felt his hand cup around my breast fondling me eagerly but gently. It was wonderful; I wanted this man to make love to me here and now. I undid my blouse and took it off, flinging it across the room. He dropped to his knees and worshipped and kissed my breasts. I was in raptures. I felt my skirt falling to the floor quickly followed by my knickers. This man had hidden talents. Within seconds I was completely naked. Once more I glanced at myself in the mirror and my heart fell with the sight of myself and I felt ashamed to be seen. 'I look terrible,' I said almost crying.

'You look wonderful. I see you not as you see yourself, but as a goddess. Do you have any dress shoes?' He asked, which surprised me.

'Yes, in my cupboard.' I said still confused.

'Put them on,' he ordered.

I opened the mirrored door and picked up a pair of shocking pink stilettos. I was about to throw them back.

'Perfect. Put them on,' he said with childish enthusiasm.

I did so and to my surprise he was right, it transformed me. The angle I had to adopt with the high heels automatically made me hold my stomach in and my chest out. However a man of his stature knew these things I do not know. I can only assume he leads a very interesting private life. I walked back to him and I could feel my tits gently sway from side to side. He obviously enjoyed the sight as he stared at them without blinking. I felt more confident and sensual now and looked at my watch which apart from the shoes was the only thing I was wearing. 'You've got fifteen minutes tiger,' I said in my sexiest voice.

Within ten seconds he was down to his underpants. He then slowly slid them down. I could see his erection bulging out of them and as he slid them down the waist band made there it stood. And what a sight it was. Large, stiff and bulbous and pulsating with desire. I wanted it in me and he could stick it anywhere. He held open his arms and I went to him. He kissed me like I had never been kissed before. He nibbled my ear and whispered.

'Kneel down.' I obeyed without question. He took his mighty cock in his hands and offered it to me.

'Now suck me.' I took it from him and let it slide into my mouth. I slowly sucked on it, letting it go in as far as I could then let it slide out my lips following every contour and particularly savouring his cock end. At last after all these years I was having warm exciting sex. I continued to work on him until he said, 'that's enough.'

He took me by the upper arms and made me stand up.

'Your turn now.' And he led me to a side desk and cleared it with one wave of his arm. He sat me on it and pushed me back so my shoulders were resting on the wall. He knelt down, parted my legs and put them over his shoulders. I could feel my lips opening in anticipation. From my knee he slowly kissed the inside of my thigh getting ever closer to my pleasure. I mentally urged him on, I wanted to be licked and sucked. As he got closer I let my fingers find my lips and pulled them open for him and I immediately felt his probing tongue arrive. He licked me into a frenzy. Then he concentrated on my clitoris and within a minute I could feel myself coming. I grasped his head and pulled him into me as hard as I could. My clitoris was in his mouth and I begged him to suck me. He did and I came in a welter of shrieks and tears of joy. It was so explosive and so sustained by his expert sucking it was unbelievable, I thought it would never stop. I sighed as my climax died down and David rose to his feet and holding my ankles high and wide his huge pulsating cock sank deeply into me. He thrust at me like a mad thing. It was wild and exciting. I could see myself in the mirror almost doubled up on the desk with David's mighty cock thrusting into my body. He thrust and thrust and my tits shook about uncontrollably, I could feel his cock deep inside me. I could not take my eyes off the image in the mirror. Those pink shoes that had caused such a transformation. David's thrusting body. I could clearly see his shaft going into me, it was outrageous, and it was pure pleasure.

I looked like a filthy back street whore that was being fucked by a trucker. And it looked and felt brilliant. I could feel David was close and I urged him on. I reached down and grasped his buttocks pulling him hard into me. 'Go on David,' I cried out. 'Fill my cunt with your hot come.' and this dirty talk did the trick. He yelled out as I felt his come shoot inside me in ecstatic pulses. It was over and what a way to finish a working day. We cleaned up using a box of tissues and got dressed with seconds to spare before the cleaners arrived.

As I drove home I realised I had left my bra behind. What must the cleaners think if they find it? Well a bad reputation is better than no reputation at all.

HOTEL STOPOVER

It was raining when we arrived at the hotel. A long journey of which we would be continuing the next part of in the morning, after our refreshing stop over. We were on our way to Mike's sisters wedding. She was thirty and had finally decided to marry her partner of eight years and go to live in France. We had left the booking of the hotel a bit late so it was very much a case of anything will do as long as it has a bed.

We parked in front of the hotel and I dashed in through the rain to announce ourselves and let Mike bring in the suitcase. The hotel was situated in a quiet part of the country, surrounded by trees and manicured lawns. An imposing gabled building of character, with old world charm. It looked very inviting and the reception was lushly carpeted and had leather armchairs strategically dispersed around a real log fire.

There was a woman sitting there with her coffee and reading the local evening paper. A rather plain looking woman, with dark hair swept back into a roll at the back and a sweep of hair across her forehead. She wore a long loose skirt and a lilac woollen pullover with an old fashioned white lace blouse underneath. Her frilly cuffs and collar contrasted rather nicely with her pullover. She was about forty I would guess, bespectacled, rather large and I have to say, with a very prominent bust. Her demeanour was one of which put me in mind of music Teacher from one of the more select girls schools. 'Good evening.' I said.
'Good evening. Rotten weather,' she replied.
I rang the desk bell and from the office at the back emerged a tall man in his late fifties. He had the look of an explorer about him, thick grey hair swept back and a well trimmed matching full beard. He was wearing a white tight fitting polo shirt which showed off very athletic shoulders and arms. He wore a pair of Lycra cycling shorts that showed off another athleticism. I could not help but look and his testicles were the size of small baking potatoes and his penis was a good seven inches long and went down the left leg of his shorts. I could clearly see the outline of a circumcised knob end and at a certain angle even the veins of his shaft. What a man I thought, if it was that length on the slack, what must it be

like when he has a hard on.

He spoke to me, but in the haze of lust it didn't register. As he moved about towards me I couldn't take my eyes off his tackle as it gently moved about within his shorts.

'Mrs Roberts?'

'That's right Sheila Roberts.' I said returning to reality.

'One night, evening meal and breakfast wasn't it?'

'Yes we're on our way to a wedding tomorrow so we thought we would break the journey so as to arrive fresh.'

'Very wise. If you wouldn't mind just filling in the details on the card.'

'Certainly.'

'Will you be joining in our activities tonight?' He said.

'No I don't think so.' Not realising what those activities were. 'But thanks anyway, we had planned on an early night.'

'As you wish, but full details of our activities are in the folder in your room so if you change your mind later you are more than welcome to come and join us.'

'Thanks,' I said politely and handing him the card.

Mike stumbled in with the suitcase and joined me at reception.

'Good evening sir.'

'Hello.'

Just then the man's wife appeared from the office door. She was of similar age and sporty persona with shortish grey hair cut into a short page-boy style. A pretty round face and a trim figure on the whole for her age. She was dressed in figure hugging grey Lycra sports trousers with a white stripe up the side. She had on a yellow vest style top that was very low cut and loose. But what spoiled an otherwise sporty image was the size of her tits. They were huge and what made them more noticeable was that she had no bra on and her nipples stood out like thumbs. Also because of their enormous size and probably years of insufficient support they sagged almost to her waist.

She seemed pleasant enough and as he reached the reception desk it seemed that she almost placed her tits on it causing them to relax and spread out sideways giving us all a good look at them. I nudged Mike in the ribs because he was standing with his tongue almost hanging out. I shouldn't be so hypocritical, because he probably thought the same about her huge tits as I did about her husband's huge cock. She continued to let her tits wallow about the desk in front of Mike with no intention of displaying any modesty.

'Room 12,' said the man.

His wife reached for the key and dropped it on the floor. On purpose, I would say, because as she bent to pick it up her tits hung down for all to see. You could see down her vest, between her tits and see the key on the floor. She recovered it, stood up, her tits bouncing everywhere. It was amazing. I had only seen two women since our arrival and they must have had a hundred and fifty pounds of tit flesh between them.

She showed us to our room and seeing her full length you had to admire the rest of her figure. Her trousers were sheer and showed her shapely legs and hips to perfection. In fact too much perfection because you could clearly see the outline of the mound and lips of her pussy. She trotted up the stairs in front of us and even from the back you could see her tits swinging about. She showed us the room and informed us that dinner would be served in about an hour, and then she departed. That gave us time to freshen up and have a drink.

We went down to dinner and Titania, whose name we had discovered on the hotel literature greeted us warmly. She escorted us to our table and we ordered drinks while we studied the menu. A few feet away behind me sat the school Teacher with another woman. I noticed as we passed them that she didn't seem the expected type of comrade. The Teacher, although very pleasant and busty, seemed plain and boring. Whereas her companion was only about five feet tall, shapely but petite and very glamorous with long flowing golden hair. She wore an electric blue one piece dress. Very low cut, making the best of a small but well cleavaged bust. It was tight fitting to show off a perfect figure and very short to show off equally perfect legs. In fact the hem just covered her knickers.

On the other side of the room I have to say was the material of my most erotic fantasies. On one long table sat fifteen gorgeous West Indian men. Fifteen Caribbean stallions I sighed silently to myself. They were all in their twenties and looked very fit and big. All were uniformly dressed in a black blazer with some sort of badge on the breast pocket, a black, blue and red striped tie. And to complete the ensemble, all wore grey flannels. What delights those trousers must contain, I mused.

My sexual daydreams were interrupted by Titania returning to take our order. I must admit that thinking about all those cocks, I hadn't really studied the menu properly. Mike ordered steak with appropriate wine and I had the same. Titania was a bit more formally dressed, in a black skirt and white blouse, which was far too tight. Again no bra and as the blouse was almost transparent, Mike was treated again to another look at her seemingly bare breasts.

The meal was delivered within fifteen minute by Titania and husband Richard together. Richard too was more formally dressed consisting of white shirt and dark tie and trousers not dissimilar to the group opposite. Again his huge cock was hanging down the leg of his trousers and because of the less restricting material was given fuller freedom. It was indeed a sight to behold watching it shake about in his left trouser leg and his balls vying for position down the other trouser leg. Even the school Teacher and her friend turned to watch the passing spectacle. I couldn't help but smile to myself when I thought about our host's names, Titty and Dick, how very apt.

It was a wonderful meal and the West Indians quietly trooped out, politely acknowledging everyone as they did so. I had assumed by the uniformity of their dress that they must be some sporting team or other. I felt my pussy getting wet again as I thought of all those lovely cocks going to waste. I did notice that they were seemed more familiar with the two ladies.

A little later I noticed Mike was eying the two women.
'I don't believe it,' said Mike.

'What?'

'That little woman with the Teacher.'

'What about her?'

'She's just shown me her pussy.'

'Don't be ridiculous,' I said.

'It's true. Look she's doing it again.'

I turned and sure enough she was turned on her chair towards Mike with her legs wide open and no knickers, showing off her pussy. Even the fact that I was looking didn't seem to bother her. What a weird collection of people I thought.

That night as we prepared for bed, I could feel heart burn coming on. 'Where's the blue bag with the indigestion in Mike?'

'Oh sorry, I've left it in the car. I meant to go back for it. I'll nip down for it.'

'No you have your shower. I'll go.' So picking up the keys and putting on the hotel complementary robe over my skimpy nightie, I crept down to the car.

There was a function room on our floor and as I approached I noticed the door was ajar and the lights on inside. I heard a slapping noise and I peeked inside. In the middle of an almost empty room was a four poster bed and at the foot end, hands manacled by chains hanging from the canopy was the little red head. She was completely naked and was been flogged with a multi lashed whip by the school Teacher, who was also completely naked. I didn't recognise her at first because she wasn't wearing her glasses and her hair had been released and hanging free. She did actually look quite attractive.

All now started to become clear to me. When Dick and Titty asked if we would be joining them for activities, this was obviously what they meant. The hotel obviously catered for the more kinky sexual appetites. Well it's a change to *Murder Mystery Weekends* I suppose. The Redhead was obviously not in any great stress and seemed to be enjoying the experience and faking agony.

'You have been an evil bitch and you must be punished.' Barked the

Teacher and flogged her again.

I jumped two feet into the air when I felt a hand on my shoulder.

'What are you doing?' Said Mike.

'You idiot. I nearly crapped myself.'

'What's going on?'

'Look for yourself.'

'Fucking hell it's an S and M session. Great.'

We watched with morbid fascination as the whipping continued and the Redhead writhed in mock pain.

'Are you going to be good girl in the future?' Said the Teacher, flogging her again.

The Teacher was far from the plain Jane that we had first encountered and Mike was obviously fascinated by this glamorous vixen. And as she whipped her victim repeatedly her huge breasts bounced about and clapped together splendidly.

'I'll be a good girl, I promise.' Cried the Redhead.

'Good,' said the Teacher lashing her again making her cry out. 'Now one last lash to make sure you do.' And she whipped her again that made her helpless victim heave back pushing her hips forward and at the same time the Teacher's tits bounce up and sideways.

'Good girls get rewards,' gloated the Teacher. 'Take her down and prepare her for pleasure.' She shouted and in walked Dick and Titty completely naked. Dicks cock swung from side to side and Titty's unfettered breasts did the same.

Dick unshackled the Redhead and took her limp body in his arms and laid her in the centre of the bed. He then shackled her wrists to chains attached to the posts at the head of the bed. At the same time Titty leaning over her with her massive tits swinging and draping over the Redheads thighs, fastened shackles to her knees so that her legs were pulled open and raised up. For the second time tonight Mike had a clear view up her pussy. The Teacher then picked up something wrapped in a towel and unrolled it revealing the biggest vibrator I have ever seen. Titty leaned over the victim's torso and reached between her legs and held the lips of her pussy open as the Teacher started to insert the vibrator.

'She'll never take all that,' I thought. But inch by erotic inch it slid inside her. She squealed and moaned in pain and pleasure as it slid ever deeper. Titty held her writhing hips as she tried to break free, her huge tits slung either side of the Redhead's waist as she held her hips forcing them onto the vibrator.

Eventually the vibrator reached the point where it would go no further and the victim gave a sigh. Titty released her grip and joined Dick who was filming the whole spectacle. The Teacher continued to work on her victim with the vibrator pushing it in and out in an ever faster rhythm. Her tits swinging back and forth as she did so. We were spell bound and watched in silence.

'Lick me, somebody lick me.' Pleaded the Redhead and Titty obliged. She leaned over her torso again and licked her clitoris as the Teacher continued to fuck her with the vibrator. Her chest started to heave and she gripped and strained on the shackles as she screamed out in an explosive orgasm.

'Wow,' gasped Mike.

The Teacher slowly pulled the huge vibrator out of the Redhead and Titty released her from the shackle. Still gasping and exhausted she slowly struggled off the bed

'Your turn now,' she said to the Teacher in a weak voice.

And the Teacher took her place on the bed. The Redhead shackled her wrists and Titty shackled her knees so her legs were wide open.

'Are you ready?' Asked the Redhead in a serious voice.

'Yes,' whispered the Teacher in a trembling voice.

The Redhead nodded to Dick who opened an adjoining door and in walked one of the Caribbean athletes. I croaked when I saw him, he was stark naked with eight inches of rock hard cock ready for action. He climbed onto the bed between her legs and without ceremony thrust his mighty shaft inside her. She let out a loud cry as he penetrated deep inside her. She gripped the chains that bound her as he continued to thrust deeply into her. Her huge firm tits going with the motion of his thrusting. With a stifled groan he ejaculated inside her, and then withdrew, and like the gentleman he was, he thanked her and left the room his massive cock deflating, swinging and dripping.

Two more entered, one of them again kneeling between her thighs and the other sitting across her waist. He grasped her tits either side of his cock and gyrating his hips back and forth he tit fucked her until he shot his load over her huge tits. They all came, either singly or in pairs to pay sexual homage to the shackled helpless Teacher. One straddled her chest and lifted her head and she took his cock in her mouth. I was astounded at how much she could take. He gripped her head and I thought she would choke, but she took it well and he came in her mouth and she sucked him dry. Some of them just jerked themselves off over her tits, which were now covered with a huge quantity of semen.

The last one was encountering a little difficulty as he had his arm in plaster. So they manoeuvred the Teacher so her bottom was at the foot of the bed. Her knee shackles were tightened to hoist her up a bit so he could fuck her standing up. This bloke had a really enormous dick, it must have been over ten inches long and he needed a bit of help. Titty obliged by leaning over the Teacher, letting her tits lay either side of her waist and holding her now very sticky cunt lips open. The Redhead took hold of the enormous dick and guided into her cunt. Her lips parted to their limit as it slowly slid in and she cried out as it went further in. Titty, who seemed to have had a lot of experience of holding cunts open for huge cocks, had a splendid view of this monster forcing its way into a tight but eager cunt. At the same time the Redhead took his buttocks and pushed him forward until the Teacher had taken his full length. The Redhead and Titty worked as a team coordinating his thrusts. On the in stroke she pushed his buttocks as Titty forced the Teachers hips hard onto his cock so it struck home on every thrust. Then pulled his hips back ready for the next stroke. It was such a tight fit you could hear her cunt squelching as a vacuum formed inside her. Then squelched again as his shaft forced its way into her tight little cunt. They looked a really erotic sight and I envied the Teacher as she was living my fantasy. Eventually the Teacher let out an unbelievable scream as she at last succumbed to an enormous orgasm that seemed to make her body shake. It was almost as if she was having a fit it was that violent and the Redhead and Titty forced the fucking couple harder and harder together. The stallion came in a welter of grunts, and such was the tight fit of his knob in her cunt, that his come cream just spurted out of her.

The show was over and as for me, my heartburn was gone but I had an aching juicy cunt that needed attention so grabbing Mikes hand we went back to bed to satisfy our lust. I pondered afterwards as to what the atmosphere at breakfast would be like.

BACK FROM OZ

We had planned to settle down and establish permanent roots now we were back in England. For the last seven years we had flitted from here to Australia to New Zealand, to England, back to Australia and now back to England again. I had met Phil on the first trip to Oz when we were both eighteen. I was doing it for the experience, a one off for a couple of years, then home to Blighty, get married and have a couple of kids. Phil on the other hand was a restless spirit who could not settle anywhere. I never really found out why but I do know he came from a troubled background. His family where all losers. His older brother and father were drunks and always in trouble with the law. His mother had a succession of fancy men and his sister was going in a similar direction.

Phil kept his emotions bottled up, he never seemed to relax. He had a skin rash that kept flaring up and when he was asleep he used to scratch his hands and would wake up sore and bleeding. I'm convinced it was all due to the internal demons, but he wouldn't get help. But this was the nineteen seventies, and we weren't enlightened about such emotional matters as we are today. But back to the seventies. Phil was getting restless again. He had, I thought landed himself a stable job at a local printers. It was within walking distance of home and he was popular with the other staff. They seemed fascinated with the stories of out travels together. We had many evenings when some of them would come around, bringing wine and beer and we all had a merry evening before they all staggered back to their cars and drove home. Again in those days there wasn't the preoccupation with drink driving as there is now.

Problem was, Phil hadn't a trade, he never stayed in one place long enough to learn one. But, he was given the opportunity of training to be a printer and I had hoped he would settle into it and become a proper tradesman. It didn't last however; he didn't want the responsibility or the hassle. That was Phil all over. He was then offered the position of van driver and this he accepted and has been doing this for six months, a long time by his standards.

But his restlessness was never far below the surface and he was itching to move again to Australia. Problem was Australia was becoming fussier. They wanted people with something to offer, with a trade at least. They did not want a freeloading whingeing Pommy like Phil. So this made him worse and more introspective. He became quiet and withdrawn.

And what about me? Well I wanted a contented husband and I didn't want to move again. We had our first child Claire who was now six weeks old and she needed stable roots. Even the arrival of our beautiful child did nothing to lift Phil's spirits, and if anything did the opposite. I think he looked upon us both as a shackle that denied him his freedom. He didn't even take notice of me feeding Claire, which was strange because most husbands take great delight in watching this wonderful event. Also we had not had sex for months. In fact thinking back his withdrawal started at about the time I announced the pregnancy. From then on he seemed cold and distant. His attitude was unexplainable. He was popular with everyone, and as I said he seemed to attract friends. So what was his problem?

Anyway Claire had been fed and changed and was now asleep so I could look forward to a few hours of quiet contemplation. It was nearly twelve thirty and Phil would soon be home for his lunch. There was a knock on the door. 'He's forgotten his key again,' I muttered to myself as I opened the door. To my surprise it was Ray. Ray was one of the printers, he was twenty one. I make that point because he spent his birthday evening with us. We knew he was coming on this particular Saturday, but we didn't know it was his birthday until he arrived. He was a very shy and thoughtful lad and some would say naive in an innocent sort of way. He had been to the house a number of times and was probably Phil's closest friend, if that is the right description because Phil seldom let people get emotionally close to him, including me.

'Ray, how nice to see you, come on in.'

'Hi Jackie. Phil's had to make a delivery to Yorkshire so he sent me round with these' said Ray as he offered me a carrier bag full of baby things.

'Oh right, thanks. Come on in.'

'What, Oh, yes,' he replied nervously and cleared his throat as he entered.

We lived in a terraced house and the front door led directly into the front room. Not an ideal situation but it would have to suffice until we were more financially settled.

'Take a seat Ray. I've just made some tea would you like a cup?'

'Yes please.' And he moved Claire's rattle as he sat down on the settee.

I went through to the kitchen and couldn't help thinking that Ray seemed a little on edge. Then I realised why. I was, shall we say casually dressed in an old white blouse with no bra, to make feeding Claire more convenient. However the milk seeping out of my nipples had caused damp patches on my blouse rendering it transparent. So Ray had had an eyeful of my nipples and it was typical of him to look away in embarrassment. I put on a cardigan to cover up the damp patches and took the tea in.

'So how are you and Yvonne getting on?' I said, placing his tea before him and sitting myself down in the armchair.

'Not too bad.'

'Any sign of wedding bells on the horizon?'

'No not yet,' he said blushing slightly.

'Well you're twenty one now so don't leave it too long.'

'No I won't.'

I had met Yvonne once and she struck me as a bit of a dull witted girl. Don't get me wrong she was pleasant and not bad looking, but vacant is the best way to describe her. I tried to visualize the two of them having sex, but somehow it didn't seem to work. Ray wasn't a bad looking lad and although five years younger than me I had to admit I fancied him. Perhaps it was his innocent charm, I don't know.

As he sat on the settee I could see the outline of his balls and cock through his trousers and he certainly looked pretty well endowed. I wonder if Yvonne had ever had that cock inside her. Or for that matter had Ray had his cock inside anyone. I felt a devilish and naughty feeling coming over me.

'How does she fuck?' I said directly and Ray's face immediately turned the colour of beetroot.

181

'I, er, oh, OK,' he blurted almost choking on his tea.

'So you have shagged her then?'

'Well er.' He squirmed in embarrassed agony. It was obvious to me that he had little or no sexual experience. I continued to probe.

'So you haven't gone all the way yet?'

'Er, no.'

'Well have you seen her naked?'

'Not exactly.'

'Well have you had your hand up her skirt?' There was silence. 'Have you had your hand in her knickers and your fingers up her pussy?' More silence. The colour of his face was returning to normal and I could see a definite bulge in his trousers. His initial shock was turning to interest as he put his hand in his trouser pocket to adjust himself. I decided to continue my line of questioning.

'Have you sucked her tits?' He remained silent and I think, nay I'm sure he was beginning to enjoy how the interrogation was going. 'Have you felt her tits?' I said gently. 'Have you even seen her tits?' Then I said in my sexiest voice. 'Would you like to see my tits?'

'Oh yes,' he pleaded.

I stood up and removed my cardigan. My blouse was still damp and transparent. I grasped it at bust level and just ripped it open sending buttons flying everywhere. Ray gasped at the sight. My tits were still full of milk and stuck out firmly. My nipples were hard and dark as was the areola ring that surrounded them. I let my skirt fall and quickly slid down my knickers. I stood naked. I let my hands follow the contours of my breasts, lifting them up and releasing them. Being so engorged with milk they didn't bounce and wobble, they just bobbed gently, a bead of milk oozing out of each nipple.

'Stand up.' I snapped. He obeyed immediately. 'Take all your clothes off.' He did so in a nervous fumbling manner. 'Quickly.' I barked. And he stood to attention completely naked for inspection. His hands were trembling slightly but his shaft did not disappoint. It was large, stiff and throbbing, and no doubt eager to give up its load. I stuck out my chest, took hold of my tits and pointed them at him. I squeezed my nipples gently, squirting two jets of milk directly into his face. The effect it had on him was interesting. He dropped to his knees and began to suck my tits. I let him indulge his fantasy for a few minutes. 'That's enough.' I said sharply. 'They are for Claire. Now sit down.' He immediately sat back down on the settee and I was enjoying immensely the power I was having over him. I wanted him to fuck me wildly, but I also knew that because of his inexperience, he would not be able to keep it up for long. I bent down in front of him and roughly opened his legs. He couldn't take his eyes off my dripping nipples. I kneeled between his thighs and took his huge cock in my hand. It was fantastically big and stiff and I let my fingers explore its length until I reached the bell shape of his knob end. It was full and purple and a little of his semen was seeping out from the end. I licked it off and it bought back memories of the early days with Phil. I took his cock in my mouth and gently sucked it. Ray moaned gently with delight and slumped back on the settee. I took his shaft further into my mouth and felt it touch my tonsils. I worked him up and down inside my mouth sucking him gently as I did so. It was not long before his heavy breathing and the pulsating of his cock told me that he was about to come. I finished him off with my hand and the timing was perfect and I pointed his cock so he would shoot his come all over my bulging tits. The strands of semen pulsed out all over them.

I was right about him coming quickly, but I also knew that he would get steam up again just as quickly. I got onto the settee to straddle him, my thighs either side of his hips. I offered him my tits and he took them eagerly rubbing them around his face. My milk was seeping out and he delved between my tits covering his face with my milk and his own come, and he was loving it. It wasn't long before he was ready and I felt his erect cock tickling my pussy. I lifted myself up and reached down to his now rock hard cock and guided it between my lips. Then I dropped down on him and I screamed out as I felt his monstrous cock slide deeply into my cunt. It was my first fuck for months and it was incredible. I rubbed my clitoris against his pelvic bone so I was being stimulated both inside and out. Rays cock was at maximum penetration and I worked us both into a frenzy of sexual joy. Back and forth I went and I could feel Rays cock waggling about inside me. That combined with my clitty rubbing against his pelvis was too much and I shouted 'Oh God I'm coming' and I could feel my eyes rolling. Simultaneously Ray half grunting and half crying also came, and I could feel his hot come shoot inside me.

What a fuck. I saw Ray again over the next few months. Eventually he did marry Yvonne and I like to think that I did my bit to get Ray into the right frame of mind for a successful sexual life. As for me and Phil, well he did eventually accept a compromise and we are still together with a second child. So alls well that ends well.

SHERRY AND CHOCOLATE

I was feeling at a pretty low ebb. Terry and I had just split up, it had been brewing for some time, we were just not a compatible match. I wanted a quiet life and he was go go go all the time. Basically I just couldn't, in fact didn't want to keep up his pace. Terry was a bass player in an up and coming rock group. They were good and were making a tidy sum from their gigs and were moving further a field to bigger venues. In fact they were on the verge of a breakthrough into the big time. It would not be fair to hold him back and in fact Terry would not be held back, and I certainly didn't want to follow him around the country. I was twenty two years old, had a university degree and had just embarked on what could be a promising career within a company of prestigious solicitors. Maybe not as exciting as life with a high flying rock band, but it could lead to a lucrative lifestyle. Anyway Terry and I parted amicably and maybe we would meet up again one day. Maybe, but I wasn't going to hold my breath as Terry was the flighty sort and I felt sure he would find plenty to occupy his thoughts and over active sexual apparatus.

I'd decided as I had the afternoon off to go and see my old college mate Kathy. I'd rang first to make sure she was in. She still lived with her Mum and Dad and as they were both at work she was at a loose end and welcomed the company. On my way there I passed the supermarket and thought to myself 'a bottle of sherry,' why not we can have one of those giggly girly afternoons comparing boyfriends and the size performance ratio of their cocks. My depression was lifting as I thought of the jollity that lay ahead.

I arrived at Kathy's and after a hug and a kiss at the door she invited me in. I held up the bottle and her eyes lit up.
'I'll get a couple of glasses,' she said as we walked into the living room, 'sit yourself down.'
A few seconds later she returned with two large wine glasses and a huge block of chocolate. The glasses were a bit big for sherry, but I thought what the hell we weren't driving. Within half an hour half the bottle of sherry and all the chocolate was gone. She went on to tell me about her

relationship with Carl with great enthusiasm.

'He was brilliant at sex, in fact the best performer I've ever known. He can keep fucking for ages without coming. I don't know how he does it, because most blokes come within a few seconds and disappear into the bathroom leaving me to finger myself off. But Carl was different; he could thrust his shaft up my cunt all night if necessary. He was a gentleman,' she said in a semi drunken slur. 'He always let a lady come first.'

'Wow,' I said.

'We've been together now for six months,' she continued 'and he had even mentioned getting married.'

'That's wonderful,' I said.

'Not really,' she sighed. 'To be honest, he is a bit too possessive, and that disturbs me.'

I couldn't help thinking to myself that this guy sounded just like what I wanted, and Kathy preferring a more exciting life would have probably got on with my ex. A pity we didn't get together earlier I thought, and then we could have made a swap. Anyway that was all water under the bridge and we continued to talk about sex and more sex.

The bottle was now nearly empty and there was talk of a few pints of her Dad's home brew. I was quite inebriated but I drew the line at home made beer. I remember with a shudder my Dad making some a few years back and remembered the ceremony of the first tasting. His comments, if I remember rightly were, 'It's not too bad after the first pint.' Then went on to sink five more pints, just to double check. The next morning he threw up every hour on the hour until mid afternoon. Then had the nerve to say, 'It must have been something I ate.'

The discussion on the merit, or not of sampling the home brew was interrupted by a knock on the door.

'Its Carl,' said Kathy pulling back the curtains.

Ah well, I thought, I've at least been spared the home brew.

She led Carl into the living room and introduced us. He seemed a little shy but a very good looking bloke. Too good for Kathy I thought. Or perhaps that's not quite fair; he just looked as though he came from a different background. Kathy offered him a glass of sherry, holding up the virtually empty bottle. He looked at the bottle held by his gently swaying girlfriend and replied, 'I wouldn't mind a coffee.'

'I think coffee would be good all-round,' I interjected, finally closing the door on the home brew debate. I also had the thought that I was being a gooseberry and decided to make an excuse to leave. 'Well maybe I'll forego the coffee till next time. I'd better be going and leave you two in peace,' I said lifting myself unsteadily from the settee.

Putting his hand on mine and looking gently into my eyes, Carl said 'No, don't go.'

The way he said it and the way he looked at me made me tingle all over and I found I could not resist his request. It was a strange feeling, but I felt a rapport with Carl, some of which may have something to do with the sexual prowess that Kathy was extolling earlier.

Some minutes later Kathy entered with the coffees and put them on a small table. She then surprised us all by taking her shirt off. She had no bra on so her large tits were indeed a sight to see. Then she slid her jeans and panties off and was stark naked. Carl, for his part just sighed quietly and smiled sheepishly at me as if this wasn't an uncommon occurrence. Putting on a disco CD, Kathy began to dance about to the beat of the music. I was half shocked and half enthralled by her performance, and was mesmerised, as was Carl by her very erotic dance routine. When her tits were not bouncing up and down and clapping together, she squeezed and manipulated them with her hands. Her body writhing with the music, her hips gyrating in simulated sexual thrusting. She gyrated over to where Carl was sitting and took his head and thrust his face into her tits. He couldn't help but respond and started to grope and suck her tits. She yelped as he bit her nipple and gently slapped his face in mock punishment. Then almost to the beat of the music she jumped onto his armchair, landing with her feet either side of Carls thighs and took hold of his head again and thrust his face into her pussy. She put her left leg on the back of his chair and thrust her hips forward, forcing his face between her legs.

'Lick my cunt you bastard' she howled, and continued to thrust her hips forward and pulling his head between her thighs. She thrust thrust

thrust in time with the intoxicating beat of the music.

I found it hard to believe what was happening but the sight was incredible, I would never think of doing what she was doing. I felt I should leave but could not as I was being drawn towards this almost ritual sex. Kathy continued thrusting her hips and pulling Carls head into her open legs. I could see his tongue licking her clitoris as she continued to urge him on. It almost seemed like she was trying to force his whole head inside her gaping cunt. Eventually she screamed out as she climaxed and her orgasm and her screaming seemed to go on and on.

I felt overawed by the situation and at the same time confused and aching for sex. What should I do? I had thought of fingering myself and make myself come, but I was too embarrassed to, and what if they saw me. The decision was soon to be taken out of my hands. Satisfied and exhausted, Kathy still had enough strength to pull me from the settee and strip me naked with in seconds. I stood there with a tingle going through my body. It was partially fear but mainly desire, sexual desire, wanton desire. Kathy kissed me passionately, gripping my shoulders. As she kissed and tongued me I felt her hands around my breasts, caressing and groping them. I felt urges welling up inside me, my pussy was glowing with desire and I could feel the moistness within. She kneeled down and sucked my nipples making them harder and longer. Rubbing her face in my tits as she had rubbed Carl's earlier, I felt her hand slide down my belly and on down between my legs. Her fingers weaving between my lips until she found my clitoris and she played with me like only a woman could. She stimulated me almost to the point, and then I felt the shock of two of her fingers shoot up inside me. She found my G spot and her fingers waggled about inside me shaking my cunt to ecstasy. Again stopping before the ultimate pleasure point. Kathy pushed me gently to the floor and I lay on a luxuriously thick white sheepskin carpet. I noticed now that Carl was naked and was about to join in. He held his mighty cock in his hand rubbing it to its full state of erection. It looked hard and massive and his huge bell end was coming closer and closer. I had a sudden qualm and felt I should get out. 'No' I cried. I tried to sit up but Kathy, who was kneeling at my head pushed my shoulders back down roughly. Carl kneeled at my feet and he lifted my legs. Kathy leaned forward draping her tits across my face to take hold of my legs. She then pulled them open so wide I was almost doing the splits on my back. I could feel my cunt was exposed and I felt my lips opening. Carl took up his position and cupped his hands around my buttocks lifting me slightly. I felt, well, I don't know what I felt. It was a combination of fear and desire and desire was winning. I reached down and found Carls massive bell end and guided it into my lips. He did the rest and his cock slid deeply into my soaking cunt. I had never been penetrated so deeply before. A combination of Kathy holding my legs high and wide and Carl lifting up my hips until my cunt was at the same level as his cock. He thrust eagerly and longingly, Kathy was right, he had supreme control of his emotion and I just relaxed and let him thrust up me until I could feel myself coming, and it wasn't long in coming. I gasped and cried as the overwhelming feeling of orgasm built up. It came slowly but surely and I could feel my whole body enjoy the experience until I just exploded into an eruption of pure ecstasy. Kathy had shuffled forward and her clit was over my face and I licked her feverously and within a few seconds she too was coming and screaming in ecstasy. Within my cunt I could feel Carl's huge cock swell up and pulsate and he too cried out as he sent a tidal wave of come rushing into my hot cunt.

What an afternoon. Since then I have always treated sherry and chocolate with great reverence and they always give me a naughty tingle.

THE END

189